Karma's Coming
Altered Karma Series Book 1
Jillian Beane

Jillian Beane LLC

ISBN: 979-8-9900-217-8-5 (eBook)

ISBN: 978-1-971038-00-1 (Paperback)

LCCN: 2025921919

Book Cover by Shawnna Sue & Jillian Beane

Editing by Dayna Hart at Hart to Heart Edits

1st edition 2025

Published By Jillian Beane LLC

Contents

Chapter 1

Karma

10 years post-earthquake

It all started with an earthquake. Not just any earthquake. *The earthquake.*

Ten years ago, when the floor of her trailer shook for the first time, Karma's world began to crumble right along with it.

The Fairway Fault Line shouldn't have existed. It was in the center of a tectonic plate, so it never should have happened. But when it did, it shook the entire continent. Rumor had it that it caused the eruption of a super volcano on the west side of the plate it occupied, but communication within, or outside of Fairway, ceased to exist in a single moment. Church bells rattled thousands of miles away to the north-east. What the mainshock didn't destroy, the nine months of aftershocks slowly whittled away.

Chaos reigned. The few bridges remaining after the mainshock were unsafe for travel and slowly crumbled into the rivers they spanned as aftershocks continued. In some spots, roads were split. Underground gas and waterlines were sheared off. Getting basic supplies to those at or near ground zero became impossible. Radar was disrupted all along the region.

Once the heart of the great continent, it was now a forgotten wasteland no one dared enter.

One company crawled to the top, providing much-needed supplies to the areas affected: Phoenix Corps.

Ten years ago, Phoenix Corps called for skilled, able-bodied men to help rebuild the city. Dorian, Karma's husband, had answered the call.

Ten years ago, he left for the job. Ten years ago, he didn't return.

Karma had done what she could to survive since then. She learned to cobble things together, forage for food, hunt, and trap. She didn't have time to feel lonely; she didn't have time to cry.

At almost forty years old, she was the mother hen of the ragtag group of people still living in a broken-down trailer park.

A startled cry caught her attention. Karma shifted her gaze to the broken window of the long-ago looted grocery store. The emptied shelves tossed askew, and scorch marks on the walls and ceiling revealed evidence of a long-ago fire. She crept in through the broken glass, careful of the sharp edges, and entered the darkened room. The familiar whimper ratcheted up her anger, but Karma tamped it down. She needed to keep her head on straight and her emotions out of it if she wanted to get Lily out of whatever trouble she'd managed to find this time. It seemed her survival lessons weren't enough to keep the orphaned teen out of trouble.

Karma skittered across the floor to the closest wall and climbed one of the few still-standing shelves. Her night vision, worse now than before, made seeing anything inside the darkened building a challenge. She focused on what she could smell. Old smoke, dirt, and dust were the dominant scents, but she could smell Lily's fear and the musky scent of feline...

When she went to Phoenix Corps one year after Dorian disappeared in desperation, starved and hurting, she was looking for help, for food. They made signing up easy. The woman who interviewed her appeared to be grandmotherly and genuine. Karma only thought her life since the quake had been a nightmare. Phoenix Corps showed her what true nightmares were.

The utopia promised, if she signed their contract to work, seemed too good to be true. She'd be provided with a comfortable apartment, meals, free medical care, and a generous stipend for other items. The sweet old woman explained that she would undergo a battery of tests to determine her strength and skills. From there, she'd be placed in one of their work programs. She'd struggled for so long. The prospect of not being solely responsible and having her needs provided for was far too tempting. She signed on the dotted line.

If she was being truthful, she also signed because she wanted to see if she could find Dorian. They'd been happy. Why would he sign up and never return? Had something happened to him? Why hadn't Phoenix Corps contacted her?

When they refused to let her return to her trailer for her meager belongings after she signed, she should've known something was wrong. Three unnaturally large men entered the room before the ink dried. She never saw the fabled apartment. Instead, she was dragged to a lab, surrounded by people in white coats and surgical masks. They strapped her to a table and drew vial after vial of her blood, so much that she was lightheaded by the time they shoved her into a room with white, padded walls and a prison-style cot. The stainless-steel toilet and sink were within reach of the door, which had a metal slide midway up.

By day two, she'd lost her voice from screaming. Her hands were bruised and bloodied from pounding on the white steel door, which sported brown, dried blood stains. No one came. No one cared. Once she stopped screaming, she could hear other newcomers. Like her, they'd scream for a couple of days, then resign themselves to their fate, and the halls would be quiet until the next victim.

There were no windows in the room, only noisy fluorescent lights that were never shut off. With no way to discern one day from the next, Karma had no idea how long she'd been trapped in that room before the same three men lumbered through her door and pinned her to the floor, zip tying her wrists and ankles. The bruising force with which they slammed her into the ground knocked the wind from her, and she struggled to breathe, sparkles dancing in her vision.

One roughly jerked her to her feet, while the second grabbed her long, dark hair and yanked back, shoving a pill into her mouth. His meaty hands clamped her mouth shut and pinched her nose, refusing to let go until she swallowed the pill. The brute's sleeve rode up to the middle of his forearm in her struggles, revealing a tattoo emblazoned on the inside of his wrist.

The stylized letters matched the innocent and heroic logo Phoenix Corps showed to the world. The added markings resembled some sort of animal print.

The third brute jammed a long needle into her hip while she was focused on the man in front of her. Her vision faded to black.

...Karma shook away the unwanted memory the feline scent—an Altered—triggered as it threatened to overwhelm her.

"I won't hurt you." The deep voice penetrated the silence of the store.

Lily whimpered again.

Karma climbed down onto the floor, using the fallen shelves for cover as she made her way silently across the floor.

Lily repeatedly stomped on the top of her captor's foot, wildly swinging her arms, trying to hit him. The man, however, was unfazed by the attack.

Karma's hand brushed against a small piece of metal, a shelf clip, and curled her fingers around it. She tossed it, its clinking sound drawing Lily's assailant's attention, while also alerting Lily.

Karma burst from her hiding spot and hurled herself at the assailant, knocking Lily away and driving her shoulder into the man's ribs. At barely five feet tall, Karma was outmatched in height, but her weight packed a punch.

The moment Lily was free and heading for the exit, Karma backed away, her eyes never leaving her threat.

The man shook his dark hair out of his eyes. Like a cat, his eyes seemed to glow an eerie green in the darkness. Shoulders rounded and back arched like a cat, he prowled forward, stalking her every move.

The musk smell in the room intensified, threatening to choke her.

"Didn't your mother teach you not to touch girls without their permission?" She backed up another step and nearly stumbled as her heel hit a toppled shelf.

"Don't you know you shouldn't run from predators?" he countered. Karma heard the smirk in his voice more than she could see it on his face.

Karma spun and lifted the entire section of shelves, hurling it at the man. Scrambling over the rest of the shelving, she was out the door, grabbing Lily by the waist, lifting her as she sped down the road, and swerving into the closest alleyway. She tossed Lily up, making sure she'd grabbed onto the rusty metal fire escape and hastily climbed up the wall until she could grasp onto it too.

With their combined weight, the bolts and the building groaned.

"Get to the top. Watch for soft spots in the roof. Make your way to the other side. There should be a matching escape there." Karma stopped moving and turned, watching for the man. Her hearing had suffered along with her vision from the experiments performed on her; very low- or high-pitched sounds didn't register to her ears any longer. The rancid smells from rotting trash and human refuse in the alley clogged her nose, making the one improved sense she had useless. She waited with bated breath.

When he still didn't appear, Karma scaled the fire escape as quickly as she could. She picked her way across the roof, avoiding the worst spots, leaping away as one area gave way beneath her. Adrenaline surging through her veins, she peered over the side of the building.

Lily stood frozen on the lowest section of the fire escape, midway down the building. Huge chunks missing from the brick below told the story of the old fire escape, now long gone. Lily's eyes were wide with terror as she gripped the railing with white-knuckled hands. The bolts above her creaked and cracked, separating millimeter by millimeter from the building, and the man with glowing eyes stared at her from below.

"In, Lil!" Karma screamed from her position.

Lily's terrified eyes met hers. She didn't move.

Karma forced her voice to soften. "Kick in the glass. Get off the escape."

Lily blinked at her.

"Lil, like I showed you." She nodded her head once. "You can do this."

Lily blinked once, twice, then shook her head and kicked with her heavy boots, splintering the glass of the window at her level. She kicked again and dove through, as the fire escape crashed to the ground.

Karma sucked in great gasps of air, turned, and raced for the rooftop door. She leapt over the rotted section of roof in front of the door, slamming her shoulder into the old wooden door, which happened to be one of the only solid things left in the building. The hinges groaned, but didn't give way, and Karma slid down the door, through the rotted roof, and into nothing.

Chapter 2

Karma

Karma grappled with every wire, pipe, and joist she encountered as she fell. All of it crumbled away as she hit, until she'd gone at least four floors. She caught a joist under her right arm. Her legs dangled through the ceiling. Plaster dust, old dirt, and construction debris rained around her, falling through the hole and down, down, down. She was above a stairwell.

Lily's gasp from below drew her attention. She stood on the landing, just emerging from one of the doors on the floor.

Karma followed Lily's gaze to the glowing green eyes at the bottom of the stairs. "Fuck." Those eyes of his were captivating. She shook off the unwanted sensation, concentrating on the threat he posed.

Slowly lowering her body until she hung by her hands, Karma kicked her feet, widening the hole. Debris rained down on the man at the bottom. She swung her feet back and forth, gaining momentum. She let go, twisted her body, and landed beside Lily. One of her feet plunged through the floor of the landing, knocking her off balance. Dragging her foot back up, Karma pulled Lily behind her as the man stalked up the stairs. The only saving grace she could hope for was that the stairs below were missing two entire sections.

Karma wiped blood from her mouth.

"You already took everything I caught! Take it and go!" Lily yelled, her voice cracking, betraying her fear. "Leave us alone!"

His eyes, still reflecting the little bit of light from various holes in the walls and ceiling, glowed eerily. He paused at the end of the last stairs in his section and made the impossible leap, catching the lowest section. With ease, he pulled his body up onto the stairs and resumed his stalking.

Keeping Lily behind her and her eyes on the man, Karma walked backward, following the wall, pushing Lily until they were back on the side of the building with the most fire escape left. She kicked a door open and shoved Lily inside, back toward the windows. "Get out. Get back to the others. I'll catch up when I can."

As soon as she was out the window, Lily raced to the bottom-most level, then dropped to the ground and took off running.

Karma turned to face those unusual eyes once more. "Took her catch, did you?"

He cocked his head to the side, his midnight hair fanning over his forehead with the movement, looking at her as if she was a puzzle he needed to figure out.

She schooled her features, not giving anything away.

He shrugged. "I'm hungry."

"Welcome to my world, asshole. You shouldn't take food from kids." Karma shifted her stance. She could dive out the window or charge him with a simple shift of her weight.

"You're not a kid."

"You didn't trap *me*. You trapped a kid." The longer she kept him talking, the longer Lily would have to get away.

He prowled closer. His unbuttoned flannel shirt caught in a breeze from the open window; his black t-shirt underneath molded to his flat abdomen. At each step, his threadbare and faded jeans accentuated the powerful muscles they otherwise hid from view. If he wasn't such an asshole, she might admit just how attractive he really was.

Karma lowered her center of gravity.

He reached forward, grabbing her arm.

Karma ignored the powerful zing pulsing up her skin at their first contact, skin to skin, his hand grazing hers. She twisted at the last minute, and he only managed to snag the sleeve of her long-sleeved shirt. She sneered at him, grabbed his sleeve, and kicked. The sound of tearing fabric echoed through the otherwise empty room.

As his arms windmilled and he stumbled back from the force of her kick, she caught the blur of a marking on his forearm. Similar to the one that marred her own skin, but different, confirming what she already suspected—he was Altered. He hit the floor hard on his butt, the floor giving way and trapping him with his arms and shins above the floor, but his torso and thighs hanging below.

She spun on her heel and dove out the window Lily used. As she raced down the fire escape, it groaned and shuddered under her weight, ripping away from the wall when she leapt from the last level remaining. It crashed to the cracked and pitted asphalt below, barely giving her time to tear her leg from the area in time.

Shards of metal and brick exploded into the air, becoming shrapnel and embedding themselves in the debris and remaining walls of the alleyway, embedding themselves in her. Damnit.

Ignoring the burning in her calf and hip, Karma fled down the alley and into the streets, using whatever debris she could find for cover, glancing behind her every few seconds to make sure the man wasn't following her.

She raced down street after street, zigging and zagging randomly, retracing and crossing her other tracks, taking the longest route possible. All the while, she watched behind her, making sure she hadn't been followed.

When the trailer park came into view, Karma huddled behind one of the first trailers, barely more than a rusty metal shell anymore, to wait and watch. She sat there catching her breath and looking for the man she'd encountered, while pulling shards of metal and brick from her legs. Time ticked by, but she wanted to be sure he hadn't followed her before returning to Lily and the others.

By the time all the shrapnel was removed and the bleeding stopped, she was fairly sure he'd given up the chase.

She pulled up her pant leg and checked her wounds, shaking her head at the chainmail-like plates now visible under the breaks in her pale skin. As she ran her fingers over the osteoderms, her fingernails clicked audibly against them. She gritted her teeth and wrinkled her nose. Damnit! She'd gone so long without injury, and now it would take months before those damn scales would be fully covered over with opaque skin again.

Pulling her pant legs back down, she looked at her now exposed left arm. He'd torn one of her favorite shirts, too. The tattoo on the inside of her wrist mocked her, moving and shifting with each movement of her hand, but it would never go away. Phoenix Corps. Those bastards had altered her, fundamentally.

Andrew Phoenix, philanthropist. He'd promised to bring in food and supplies, to deliver to those most in need. The company would provide construction supplies and build crews from strong, able-bodied men to offer not only jobs, but also relief and the ability to rebuild some of what they had lost.

The bastard did none of the things he promised. The able-bodied men disappeared. The buildings were never rebuilt. Food was only given to those Phoenix Corps deemed worthy. Or those who signed their lives away under a pretense of aid, only to be tortured and tested on—to be made into monsters.

She tipped her arm this way and that. The ink had a shimmery quality to it, catching what little light fought its way through the permanent dust cloud hovering over the area.

When she'd first escaped from Phoenix Corps, she'd tried to cut it out, along with the tracker they'd embedded. While she'd successfully managed to dig the tracker out from deep in the muscle of her left deltoid, dulling several knives to cut through the tough scales beneath the surface of her human skin—that damn ink shimmered on her scales too. She still cringed at the remembered pain from skinning the osteoderms from her sensitive inner wrist, only to have those regrow and the ink bleed back up to the surface, mocking her. She didn't understand what they had done, how they had done it, but the tattoos were impossible to remove. No one would ever call her a genius; street smarts were her strength. But if she ever figured out how to undo what they'd done, Karma would jump at the chance.

She shook her head and stood.

It was there forever. Just like the scales beneath her human flesh and the abnormal strength she had for her size, she'd be living with the consequences of going to Phoenix Corps for help for the rest of her life. Karma looked around, making sure no one was in sight, stood, and backtracked the last half mile. If the man was going to catch up with her, he should have by now. She wouldn't rest until she knew for sure. Endangering the people in her care wasn't an option. She'd worked too hard and too long to build the sanctuary here at the trailer park. No one would mess that up for her, especially not another Altered.

Karma jogged past some signs, long overgrown with weeds and vegetation, using them for cover. The few bits of buildings in this area were slowly being consumed by the plants and earth around them. It left her with good cover, but it was dangerous, especially in the waning light, because deep holes and sharp edges were hidden by the very vegetation useful for hiding in. One bonus of this extra precaution—she could check her traps and hopefully bring back dinner to the others.

She couldn't smell the musky scent of the Altered man. Taking another roundabout way, she entered the trailer park from the other end, meandering around in circles to mask her trail if he happened to catch up. Satisfied, she headed to the center of the park, where Lily and the rest of the people who relied on her were.

Entering the trailer she'd shared with Dorian so long ago, Karma trailed her hand over the kitchen countertop she'd so lovingly refinished. It was now cracked and worn, and as usual, devoid of food. No lanterns were lit in this room or the next. Going more from memory than sight, Karma walked down the hallway and hung a right, pushing at the faux wood paneling and opening a door into an addition she'd built on. This one was a glorified hallway, too. The walls, if there'd been enough light, would display drawings done by the kids over the years, using the charcoal left over from a fire they'd cooked over. She stepped down onto the ground she'd leveled and painstakingly covered with paneling she'd robbed from a few other trailers in the neighborhood.

Pushing through another door, she entered the side of a neighboring trailer and down its hallway, into the kitchen. She pushed the rag rug aside and lifted a panel in the floor. The darkness hid the stairs she'd carved into the earth. Karma bent as she closed the hidden panel again and made her way down the tunnel. Her increased strength and sudden talent for digging allowed her to carve out this tunnel and the room it led to. She trailed her hand down the walls and ceiling, checking for places in need of repair. Finding none, she knocked twice on the makeshift door at the end and pushed it off to the side.

Warm light, made brighter by the pitch dark she'd just traversed, poured through the doorway. A threadbare couch, scavenged from another trailer, and army-style cots lined the room. They'd made cheerful rag rugs and hung them around the room, making the dirt and stone walls a bit less stark, and helping to insulate them. Old plastic bags they'd found and scavenged were woven into mats to cover the floors.

Lily rushed to her side. "Are you okay? What happened to the guy? Did you kill him? I'm sorry I lost the catch!" The words spewed from her mouth at an alarming rate, too fast for Karma to answer anything, as Lily just kept going.

The others joined in, asking their own questions. Karma lifted her hand to stop them all. Three fairly large rats hung from her hand. She tossed them to Lily. "Clean these. Don't light any lanterns on the way. Leave the guts in the canister in the kitchen. I'll take care of getting rid of them in the morning." She dropped her hand to Peter's perpetually mussed, light brown hair.

He was a few years younger than Lily, around thirteen years old.

"Help her cook them. Keep the blinds closed. I covered my tracks. The other Altered shouldn't be able to find us here, but be cautious, just in case."

"He's still..." Lily started, her voice trailing off.

"Alive? Yes. I didn't kill him." Karma placed her hand on the young girl's shoulder. "You and I will work more on your defense techniques tomorrow. You did well. If he'd not been Altered, you most likely would've gotten away from him."

"If he goes back to Phoenix and tells them about you, about us..."

"We'll deal with that when the time comes. For now, dinner."

Lily nodded. Her short blond hair flapped with the motion, and she waved for Peter to enter the tunnel, scooting around him to take the lead once inside.

Rosie sat on the threadbare couch watching their interaction, but her fingers never stopped moving as she worked to weave another plastic mat. Rosie was a friend of Mrs. Thorn's, the neighbor who'd once lived in the trailer they now lived under. When Mrs. Thorn fell ill a few years ago, they'd invited Rosie to live there and help care for her and the others while Karma was out catching and trapping food or scavenging.

Rosie's graying strawberry hair was kept short, her natural curls standing up in all directions. In recent years, she'd become sicklier. Her skin had taken on a grayish tinge, and she found herself out of breath very easily. Luckily, it had been years since Karma had stumbled on a young child needing care, and most of her charges were self-sufficient now, or they'd left the area. Lily and Peter were the youngest remaining. Several others were living in other trailers in the compound, able to fend for themselves. Their little community had grown over the last six years since she'd escaped the clutches of Phoenix Corps, but everyone kept to themselves.

Chapter 3

Karma

The wind-up alarm clock buzzed angrily. And just as angrily, Karma slammed her hand onto it, silencing it. She'd spent most of the night dreaming of the eerie, glowing eyes of the man from yesterday.

The others stirred as she rolled out of her cot, her joints aching from the long falls she had taken the day before. She stifled a groan when the enormous bruise on the underside of her upper arm protested loudly.

She jammed her feet into her shoes and headed up into the trailers. Karma needed coffee. But since that was no longer an option, she needed to make her brew from the dandelion roots she kept stockpiled in the trailer. One thing about that hardy weed, it could even grow here. Apparently, dandelion coffee was better nutritionally. "*Nutrition my ass*," she muttered to herself.

She downed the mixture when it was ready, wishing for the caffeine kick of real coffee, then washed up her metal "mug" and placed it back in the cabinet with the others.

Canned goods served multiple purposes now. Not only did it provide food, but the can could then be washed up and used for dinnerware. She kept a substantial collection of them, and Lily and Mrs. Thorn made small rag weavings as can cozies, so the can wouldn't burn skin when it contained something hot.

"Where are we headed this morning?" Lily asked, coming down the hallway.

"*I'm* headed out to see what I can find to eat today. I want *you* to stay here with Peter and Rosie."

Lily looked hurt. "I didn't mean to mess up yesterday..."

Karma walked over and tilted Lily's chin down, so their eyes met. "You didn't mess up. That guy was an Altered. If it had been a regular guy, you would've easily gotten away, and probably with the food." She gave her a quick hug. "This isn't punishment. I have some things to do today. I need you to stay here. Okay?"

Lily nodded, appeased for the moment.

"Work with Peter. See if you guys can find some more dandelions in the compound. We are starting to run low."

"You know that's more like tea than coffee, right?" Lily teased.

"Hush. I get so few pleasures. Leave me my delusions!" Karma shrugged on her black leather coat over her black, long-sleeved shirt. "It'll be an unusually chilly one today. Stay close to Peter and within the compound."

Lily saluted as Karma walked out the door.

When she walked out the door of the trailer, Karma was instantly alert. In the last year, she'd been a little less paranoid of Phoenix Corps trying to find her. After the encounter with the Altered the day before, she was back to being paranoid. Her eyes darted from trailer to trailer, looking for anything out of place. Her nose on alert, she sniffed at the air but found no unusual smells. Still, she crept from place to place, scanning her surroundings and waiting for the boogieman to jump out from every darkened corner.

The moment the trailer park was out of sight, she relaxed a bit. The further away, the less likely someone she stumbled on could associate her with it. Keeping its location quiet kept the others safe.

Approaching town, she crept down an alleyway, then climbed a crumbling wooden fence. Up and over, then down another street. She crossed the road, oblivious to the weeds and vegetation pushing through the crumbling asphalt, growing around long-abandoned cars. Their paint was sun-bleached, and orange-brown stains surrounded the vehicles' footprints where the acidic water from the rain had run over the rusted metal, leaving a creepy chalk-like outline. She vaulted over the last car, down another alley, and up to the more recently constructed brick wall.

She scaled the wall, then hanging from the top by her arms, peered over. The steel and glass structure stood gleaming, even with the overcast sky. A stark contrast to the decaying cityscape behind her, this building was state-of-the-art, clean, and well-maintained. It looked like any office building from before. But she knew the nightmares it held inside.

Karma released her hold on the wall and dropped back to her feet. Hightailing it out of the alley, she darted down the next street and into what used to be a popular park. For a long time after the quake, someone had been coming to the park and keeping the benches free of the creeping vines that seemed to cover every available surface. But a few years ago, that stopped. The person either died or became a victim of Phoenix Corps, or both, and no one else took up the mantle. Bench-shaped greenery dotted what used to be a lovely path. She followed that path now, weaving around and through the benches, veering off only when the path reached the trees.

There was no discernible path through the trees, but Karma knew the way. She plowed through the bramble bushes, ignoring their grip on her jeans. The trees ran right up to the electrified fence, and beyond. Despite the electricity running through the chain-link, foliage covered it from top to bottom, insulating her from the worst of the shock when she spread the opening she'd made long ago. The arrogant idiots running the facility still hadn't figured out how Karma had escaped six years ago.

On their side of the fence now, she hugged close to it, staying within the cover of the trees until she was near the gate. Once the next supply truck was inspected and allowed to pass, Karma dashed by the guard shack, while they watched the next truck driving in.

Karma sped past the rear axle of the box truck and dove under, gripping the undercarriage and hanging on as the truck followed the road and into the loading dock.

She nearly lost her grip when the truck slammed to a sudden halt. The driver shouted at the dock workers to "Hurry up with the damn door!" She readjusted her weight and waited. A moment later, a screech pierced the air, followed by the clinking of chains.

The driver stepped down from the truck, his steel-toed boots coming into view as he grunted at some of the workers and screamed at others. They disappeared again when he jumped onto the tailgate. She used the sound of the door rolling up to mask any sound as she dropped to the floor and rolled away from the voices.

She'd done this routine a number of times, usually to pilfer food. Karma slipped around a corner quickly, barely avoiding the rotating camera there. She slipped into the closest office and grabbed a dock worker's coat from the racks along the wall.

It was so weird that it was easier to break into this place during the day than at night.

She tugged on an old Fairway Falcons hat. Back before the quake, the Falcons had been her husband's favorite baseball team. Her long hair, a strange brownish-gray the color of a Komodo dragon's scales, tucked easily inside the overly large hat. She grabbed a clipboard from the stack sitting on the desk, tucked it into her arm, and hurried back out into the hall.

Keeping her head down, Karma walked into the empty box of the truck at the end like she was checking to make sure they got it all. She turned on her heel, clomped back out, and turned, heading down the next hallway. She tossed her dock coat into the nearest trash can, quickly picked the lock of the next office, and darted inside.

The pungent smell of salt water and too much cologne, but somehow not enough to cover the body odor, made her nostrils burn and her eyes water. Great. Pip was here. From the strength of the stench, he'd not been out of the room long.

She reached into the cabinet and yanked out a lab coat, throwing it on over her leather jacket, and tromped back out into the hallway.

Halfway down the hall, the hair on the back of her neck stood on end. That scent. The Altered from the night before was here somewhere. Questions swirled in her head. He had been alone. Goon squad members were rarely out of the compound alone. And he was scavenging for food. He shouldn't have been going hungry if he worked for Phoenix Corps.

Karma followed her nose.

She turned right, heading down one of the other offshoot hallways, and heard muffled sounds of struggling behind the second door she came to. This room was a torture chamber for those who'd run.

Another grunt caught her attention from inside the room, and the repeated snap of flesh meeting flesh. Was the Altered with those mesmerizing green eyes doing the beating? Or was he the victim?

She flexed her fingers, indecision wracking her. Her hand shook. Memories of the condition she was in when they removed her from that room flooded her. No one deserved that.

The loud thuds echoed through the hallway as her fist pounded on the door, the way she remembered Pip pounding on it that day, so many years ago.

The handle lowered, and a deep baritone voice emerged. "We're not even close to being done!" The blond brute didn't even bother to look out the door as he spoke.

Karma snapped her foot out, catching the brute in the back of the knee. She stepped closer, slamming her elbow into the junction between his neck and shoulder at the same time as his knees hit the floor. The snap of his collarbone reverberated up through her arm, and his eyes rolled back into his head, falling face-first onto the tiled floor.

He'd only be unconscious for a minute. She needed to move quickly.

The Altered strapped to the inverted table in the center of the room was the green-eyed man from the night before. Bruises marred his handsome, chiseled face. His t-shirt was ripped, and she could see ugly bruising beginning and a gash with pitch black fur peeking through.

Karma pulled the table upright and tore at the straps holding him in place.

The man stumbled forward, then shoved her to the side, driving his shoulder into the brute who was back on his feet and raging. The two of them crashed into the door.

The brute drove both of his elbows down, aiming for Mr. Green-eyes' spine, but he shifted, taking the blow to the back of his ribs instead. The hit drove Mr. Green-eyes to his knees, but he grabbed the brute's ankle, tripping him up as he lunged for Karma.

Grabbing one of the steel batons kept on the counter in the room for the punishments dispensed in this room, she whipped her arm out, extending it to its full length. She ignored the pain from her ankle and brought the baton down as hard as she could across the back of his neck. The sickening crack told her she didn't need to worry about him getting back up.

Karma stepped forward and helped Mr. Green-eyes to his feet. His breathing was labored, and he couldn't straighten. At least a couple of his ribs must have been broken with that hit he took.

"You want out of here?" she asked.

The incredulous look he gave her made her smile.

"Just checking." Karma poked her head out of the door. The corridor was empty. "Can you walk?"

He straightened a bit and nodded.

"Stay in front of me, like I'm escorting you to another room. I've got a couple of stops to make and then we'll be out of here."

Karma's pulse jumped, not entirely from fear as they entered the hallway. The view of him from this angle wasn't bad either. She shook off the thought. She needed to pay attention to the things around them, not the man in front of her.

They backtracked to the hall outside Pip's office and continued down the hall where she had been before she'd gotten distracted by Mr. Green-eyes' scent.

She pushed lightly on his shoulder, directing him through the set of double doors in front of them. She immediately darted through the next door they came to—a storage room, filled to the ceiling with cans of food. Taking a precious moment, she stuffed as many cans as she could fit into the canvas bag she kept on her.

Once the bag was full, she dropped the clipboard and grasped one of the skinnier cans in her hand. It wasn't brass knuckles, but it would have to do. Afraid speaking would draw attention, she pointed at the door with her free hand, and then in the direction she planned to take him.

There were some muffled sounds she could make out, but nothing she could distinguish. She hesitated, laying her empty hand on the paddle handle of the door. Taking in a deep breath, she pushed the handle down and pulled the door toward her.

Pip walked right into her.

Taking advantage of his surprise, Karma reared back with the hand holding the can and punched, putting all her significant power behind it. An audible crack sounded when her fist connected with Pip's cheek.

The skin on his face tore, as did the skin on her knuckles. She felt the sound down to her knees as her osteoderms skidded over his dermal denticles, the tooth-like scales under his skin, grinding against the rough bony texture of hers.

The surprise wiped away from his face, and his abnormally wide mouth gaped in a grotesque smile, showing the triangular, serrated rows of teeth occupying that space.

Karma lifted her other arm to block him as Pip dove at her, mouth-first. He bit her forearm, his teeth easily penetrating the linen of the lab coat, the leather of her jacket, and the cotton of her shirt, digging through her thin human skin and into the osteoderms below. She stifled her cry of pain when he ripped his head back and forth, attempting to rip the flesh from her bones, like his wild counterpart would've done. Rearing back with the can again, she aimed for his eye, landing the blow three times before Pip flinched and released her.

Blood oozed down her forearm. Karma lifted her booted foot and shoved Pip away from her, across the hallway, and into the opposite wall.

"Pet, I feel your heart racing," he taunted, tapping his forehead and the bridge of his nose, where pockets of gel under his skin picked up on pulses of electricity and sent the message to his brain.

"What is it like to have more teeth than brain cells, Pip? I'm surprised you haven't been bouillabaisse'd into shark fin soup. At least then you'd have a purpose."

His eyes glazed over, fury pumping off him, and he dove at her again. Pip's jaws locked onto her side. The air rushed out of her lungs.

Karma dropped to her knee, raising her hand with the can, repeatedly jamming it into his eye socket. She couldn't pull in a full breath, and she began to feel lightheaded. She regretted her next move before she took it. She let her own serrated teeth, which hid in pockets of her gums behind her human teeth, emerge. She latched onto his arm, pumping venom and bacteria into the bite. She fought back the bile rising in her throat at his overripe smell and clamped down harder.

Her venom caused cramping, nausea, and difficulty breathing, but Pip didn't seem to be slowing down.

Pip's jaw tore from her side.

Karma dropped to her other knee, doubled over, gulping in air.

Pip screamed in frustration, causing her to look up and see Mr. Green-eyes rake his claws across Pip's chest. He dodged Pip's attempt to bite him, side-stepping and slashing vicious claws down Pip's back, kicking him away. He turned to look at Karma, and before she could shout a warning, Pip clamped down on Mr. Green-eyes' shoulder, Pip's teeth sinking in deep.

Karma grabbed her canvas bag by the handle and swung as hard as she could, slamming the bag into Pip's face.

Pip's teeth released Mr. Green-eyes, his eyes rolling back in his head. Blood spurted from the wound on Mr. Green-eyes' shoulder. Shit. Pip must have nicked an artery.

Karma closed the distance and clamped her hand over the wound, applying pressure.

He stumbled into her, his eyes getting a glassy, glazed-over look.

She threw the long handles of the canvas bag over her shoulder, then shifted, wedging her shoulder under his, keeping pressure on his wound.

"Ok, Green-eyes," she put command in her voice, "You need to stay awake until we get out of here. Once we're in the clear, then you can pass out. Got it?"

He grunted.

Instead of going back the way she'd entered, Karma stepped around Pip and pushed her way through the next door. The hallway was blissfully empty. Picking the lock to the next storage room one-handed took longer, but she still managed, thankful for her dexterity. Dragging Mr. Green-eyes with her, she shut the storage room door and propped him up against the wall. She turned on the light long enough to check his wound. It was healing, slowly.

Black fur poked through the punctures in his human skin. She grabbed gauze and bandages off the wire rack. She packed the gauze around the worst of his wounds and wrapped the bandages tightly. She threw extras into the canvas bag with the food, then turned, dismantling the shelf to jam the door's paddle handle. It was going to take a lot of work to get through that door, but once someone managed, it would look like the shelf fell and blocked the door. Feeling her way to the back wall of the storage room, she found the heavy chest freezer with the padlock.

Karma grabbed one end, hefting the load up onto its edge, and twisted, walking it a few feet from the wall. Behind it gaped a hole in the concrete block wall. Her ability to dig had come in handy more than just for the tunnels under the trailer park. She turned and gathered Mr. Green-eyes, shoving him into the hole as the commotion ramped up in the hallway. They didn't know which room she'd gone into from the sounds of it, but she didn't want to stick around until they found her.

She climbed into the hole after him and pulled the freezer back against the wall, being as quiet as possible.

Mr. Green-eyes didn't respond when she nudged him forward, so Karma got in his face, snapping her fingers.

"Stay with me," she said as loud as she dared. "Put your hand here." She took his hand in hers and wrapped it around her ankle. "It's too narrow and low for me to carry you, yet. Just hold on. I'll get us out of here."

She moved more slowly than she would have on her own, but they made it out of the smaller portion of the tunnel through the concrete and into the dirt, which she'd widened a bit more over the years. The maze twisted and turned, dumping them out into a drainage tube.

Karma helped him stand, allowing him to lean his weight against her as they trudged through the muck. The area lightened, the dim light of the day now visible at the other end. She walked him over to the side and propped him against the sidewall of the tunnel. He'd started to bleed through the bandages on his shoulder. She needed to get them out of the tunnel and away from this place. "I'll be right back."

Finding the tiny handholds, Karma climbed to the top of the wall and reached toward the center, grabbing the chain and pulley lodged into the ceiling. She calculated the timing, then released the lock and yanked on the chain, watching the gridded metal gate lift at the mouth of the tunnel.

She released her grip, dropping into the muck. Shoving her shoulder into Mr. Green-eyes' abdomen, she lifted him in a fireman's carry and clomped through as fast as she could. His extra weight drove her feet further into the muck than she was used to, requiring more effort to pull her feet free of the suction.

She just squeezed them through as the gate clanged shut. The locking mechanism clunked loudly.

They were on the wrong side of the service road from the park. She stayed hidden in the embankment of the drainage ditch until they were out of sight of the guards, and raced across the road, behind the rubble of a long-ago fallen building for cover.

Putting Mr. Green-eyes down, she rechecked his wound. The bleeding had mostly stopped, only oozing now, likely from the jostling he endured while she carried him. He'd either passed out or gone into the healing sleep. Exhaustion pulled at her, but she couldn't afford to sleep now. She needed to get as far away from the Phoenix Corps complex as possible before she rested. And Mr. Green-eyes wouldn't be safe here either.

As quickly as she could, she changed his bandage. With their rapid healing, he would likely be fine, but the muck in that tunnel—she wouldn't want it on *anyone*'s wounds.

Heaving him back into the fireman's carry, trying not to think of how solid his muscles were against her and ignoring the warmth seeping into her from every place they touched, Karma headed into the ruins of Fairway, back toward the one place she knew she could keep them safe, the one place she was terrified to take an unknown Altered to.

Chapter 4

Karma

Thankfully, Mr. Green-eyes didn't wake up on the way back. She was certain he would wake ready to fight, and she'd seen what kind of damage his claws could do.

As she entered the trailer park, the skies opened up. The acidity in the rain made it not a good idea to stand out there for long, especially with wounds, which nixed her idea to take him to the first trailer, which was little more than a hollowed-out shell. Gaping holes in the roof would offer them no protection from the elements. She'd have to take him to hers.

She wouldn't take him below, though.

Lily must have been waiting for her and gasped at the sight of Karma's cargo.

"I brought some canned goods. Take them down to the tunnels but leave me two." She chucked the canvas bag at Lily. "Something with meat. Then go down and stay there. Only leave and return through Mrs. Thorn's trailer. Don't come back through here after this until I say otherwise."

Lily's eyes widened, zeroing in on Karma's arm.

Four shark teeth stuck up through her jacket. She sighed. "Before you lock yourself and the others down there, bring me the tweezers from the first aid kit." She shook her head. "Eww. I've had Pip's teeth embedded in my arm for hours. Boiling it wouldn't be enough to erase the taint," she muttered.

Karma hefted Mr. Green-eyes, adjusting his weight, and turned to the bedroom opposite the hall from Lily. Taking extra care, she bent until his feet touched the floor and held him steady as she stood.

This close and with the small bit of daylight pushing through the ripped curtain on the window, she could see a subtle pattern in his dark hair. Most of it was a deep, almost bluish-black. In the darkest brown, a pattern of rosettes emerged.

She guided him to a sitting position on the edge of the threadbare cot and removed his flannel shirt, while keeping him upright. Without the flannel, she could clearly see the marking on the inside of his wrist. The mark of the altered. His were paw prints amid the P, C letters—paws with distinct claws—and the number 7619.

She laid him flat and grabbed a knife, cutting away the bandages and the remains of his shirt near his wounds. She tried not to laugh at the ridiculous asymmetrical neckline left behind.

"Is he going to one of those 'formal dances' Mrs. Thorn used to go on about from 'back in her day'? I bet we can still find one of those pictures in her trailer." Lily giggled and handed over the first aid kit.

"You'll have to make him a corsage," Karma quipped. "Now go. Off with you. I don't know when he will awaken, but it may be soon. Remember what I said. In and out through Mrs. Thorn's trailer, and *only* if necessary. The less he knows about this place, the better."

When Lily firmly closed the hidden door behind her, Karma closely examined his wounds. The punctures were mostly healed, leaving tufts of black and brown fur sticking through the breaks in his human skin. She absently wondered if it itched, having all those little hairs trapped under the skin.

With the wounds closed, she didn't need to rebandage him. Karma's eyes drifted over him. He was solidly built, strong, and handsome. Even in his healing sleep, a wildness surrounded him. His left hand lay beside him, palm up, and she could see the tips of his claws peeking up from the sheaths directly under his fingernails. The tattoo on his inner wrist shimmered in the dull light coming through the window, a warning that, like her, he was dangerous. Until she knew why he'd helped her with Pip, why he was at Phoenix Corps, she needed to remember that he was a threat.

Karma pulled the neckline of the remainder of his shirt down to expose his other shoulder. She probed the area where she'd found her tracker. Upon close inspection, a thin scar ran down his human skin, and she could feel a tougher scar beneath, in the fur layer, its presence obvious in the texture under her fingers. To be sure, she probed for the familiar shape all over the muscle there, finding it empty of the tracker's large oblong shape.

The corded muscle there was hard. Her fingers tingled at the feel of his warm skin beneath them. His face, softened with the healing sleep, couldn't hide the chiseled bone structure beneath, the powerful muscles of his jaws, the thick, dark eyelashes. His nose had a slight bend to it, likely broken at some point. Her fingers itched to run through his hair to see if the rosette pattern was softer than the rest.

Karma stood abruptly, concerned about the direction her mind had taken. She couldn't afford to be attracted to this Altered, or anyone. She had responsibilities. Their safety depended on her, and bringing in strangers put them all in danger. She knew nothing about him, other than that he stole their food, and she'd just found him in the Phoenix Corps headquarters. He may have helped her against Pip, but she didn't know why he was there.

If she wasn't careful, he could easily destroy every ounce of safety she fought so hard to build. She clenched her hands at her sides as that thought entered her mind, stealing her breath with panic.

Needing space to breathe and an extra security measure, Karma went out to the kitchen and pulled a hunk of rope from a lower cabinet. She could break the rope easily; he probably could too, but it might give her an extra second to react. Nothing in the room would be substantial enough to tie him to. She looped the rope around his wrists, wrapped it once around the metal frame of the cot above his head, then threw the rope under the cot to his feet. She tied the other end around his ankles. She kept slack in the rope so it wouldn't pull on his injured shoulder, but it was tight enough to limit his range of movement, and he wouldn't be able to untie it.

She'd just pulled the last tooth free from her arm when a roar launched her to her feet. A few quick strides and she stood in the doorway to the bedroom.

Fury flared in those green eyes as he pulled at the rope so hard the metal cot frame groaned in protest.

"You're safe," she said calmly.

"You call this safe?" he roared.

She cocked her hip, planting her fist there. "I'm not going to hurt you. I tied you up because I figured when you woke from your healing sleep, you'd be disoriented and angry. I like my limbs attached."

He cocked his head like he was listening to something.

She hoped Lily had not come running when he roared. "Last time I saw you, you stole food from a child and then proceeded to chase us. Forgive me for being wary, since our second encounter was in a facility that is responsible for the death and torture of so many."

He roared again and struggled against his bonds. "I could ask you the same question about Phoenix Corps. What were *you* doing there?"

"Grocery shopping." She held up one of the cans Lily left for her. "Hungry?"

He yanked at his arms, the ropes starting to fray.

"Look, I didn't bandage you up and carry your ass all the way out of the facility to here only for you to tear apart my belongings. I'll make you a deal. Calm down and quit struggling, and I'll untie you and feed you. Then you can go on your merry way and not darken my doorstep again. Sound like a plan?"

He made a sound she could only describe as a chuff, then nodded.

She untied his feet first.

Mr. Green-eyes burst into motion and had her pinned to the trailer wall, the frayed edges of rope still hanging from his wrists.

Karma kept still, except to lift the can into his line of sight. Her feet were at least a foot off the floor, their eyes on the same level. "Take it and go."

He eyed her, confusion marring his handsome face. The muscle around his jaw ticked as he clenched his jaw. Abruptly, he dropped her and stepped away.

She still held out the can. "You helped me when you didn't need to. Take it."

"You got me out when I was in no condition to do it myself."

She shrugged it off and tossed the can, which he easily caught. "Even so. I have enough to feed me for a while. Take it."

"What's your name?" he asked. His eyes were intense, looking through her, trying to find—what? She didn't know.

It was her turn to look at him with confusion. "Why?"

"I'd like to say thank you."

"You just did."

He shrugged. "Well, thank you then, pet." He turned and walked toward the door. He paused before leaving, his nose lifted, scenting the air down the other hallway. He gave a mysterious smile and tipped an imaginary hat. "You can call me Ridge when we run into each other again."

"Let's not run into each other, huh?"

"We'll see." He winked at her and headed into the rain, which had slowed some.

Karma ignored the fluttering in her belly at his obnoxious flirtation and slammed the door shut behind him.

Chapter 5

5713

Karma

When the rain finally stopped, hours later, Karma left the trailer. She'd instructed Lily, Peter, and Rosie to continue on as if Ridge were still in the trailer. She needed to make sure that he'd really left, and he wasn't going to come back sniffing around the compound. There were too many within the boundary of the trailer park who wouldn't be able to protect themselves from an Altered like Ridge.

The lingering dampness in the air cooled down the temperature, bringing a chill to her skin, even through her leather jacket, the new ventilation in her sleeve adding to the chill. The distinctive treads of Ridge's boots left deep impressions in the mud leading out of the trailer park and into the street beyond. He'd stopped leaving impressions, but the smeared, muddy footprints continued down the street and into an alley before disappearing altogether. The rain diluted his scent, making it difficult to follow. With both trails gone, she changed direction and headed back to the trailer park the long way.

Karma kept her eyes on her surroundings, but her mind wandered. Ridge had lost a lot of blood. Should she really have let him go yet? She didn't want to keep him around. It was too dangerous. She didn't know who he was or what his agenda was. Lily, Peter, and Rosie were her priority. She needed to keep them safe.

About six blocks away, she picked up a strange scent. Her body broke out in a cold sweat. Her heart raced. Usually, she could pinpoint where she'd first smelled a scent, but this one was different. Her instincts screamed for her to run.

Karma scurried to the shadows, behind a remaining half of a brick and steel wall. There were gaping holes in the wall where the bricks had crumbled away, exposing the rebar grid within.

Taking advantage of the holes, Karma peered down the street.

"This is stupid," The gruff voice said. "Shark-boy is just embarrassed to admit he got his ass handed to him by some dock worker he pissed off."

A brick sailed down the street, clanging loudly against an old, rusted car.

A deeper-than-usual female voice responded, "He claims it was five-seven-one-three."

Karma didn't need to look down at the numbers on her wrist. They were burned into her brain as permanently as they were tattooed on her wrist.

"If that bitch is stupid enough to be hanging around, she's got to be smart enough to steer clear of HQ. I mean, she's evaded capture this long. My money says she's either dead or long gone." Gruff guy continued as they passed the rubble she hid in, "He's had a hard-on for five-seven-one-three since before I left recruitment."

Karma carefully shifted her position, keeping out of sight, but wanting to get a better look at the Altereds searching for her. A memory tickled her brain when they turned the corner and the male's profile became visible. She swallowed bile, trying to steady her trembling hands. He was one of the gorilla-altered men who took her from the office the moment she signed over her life, for help. She hadn't encountered him since he'd helped the others to strap her to the cold, steel table in the lab where they tortured her, tested on her, and ultimately, changed her life forever.

The realization brought panic with it. The need to flee gripped her by the throat, restricting her breathing. A vise clamped around her chest, constricting her heart. Her vision narrowed. Her legs weighed tons, frozen in place.

A disembodied, feral scream tore through the air. It took too long for her to figure out it came from her own throat. She clamped her hand over her mouth to silence it, but it was too late.

The Altereds turned and raced in her direction.

She took a step backward and fell through the floor.

A strong arm pinned her against a hard body. Another hand reached up, yanking the trapdoor in the floor closed. Door closed, the same hand clamped over her mouth to keep her from screaming again, and a deep voice purred in her ear. "Stalking me now, pet?"

Karma knew that voice. His scent burned into her brain during their first encounter and was not helped by their second. Ignoring the unwanted tingles his touch caused, she stayed quiet until there was silence above. Dim lighting and her poor eyesight in the dark hid most of the room's details. She didn't want to look too closely at the fact that his mere presence ratcheted down her anxiety. She'd never picked up Ridge's scent, even standing right above the trapdoor she'd just fallen through. His scent surrounded her now.

At the first sign the Altereds were gone, Karma struggled against his hold, but he had her locked in tight. Using her human teeth so he didn't get a dose of venom, Karma bit down on the meat of his hand.

"Ouch! I just saved your ass."

"Don't. Call. Me. Pet." She punctuated each word with a hit from her elbow, heel, fist, and knee, shoving him away from her. She connected hard enough to move him away from her, but not enough to hurt him.

Ridge put his hands up in surrender. "You didn't give me a name, sweetie. I'll use nicknames until you give me one."

"Didn't anyone ever tell you that curiosity killed the cat?"

"Didn't anyone ever tell you that introducing yourself is the right thing to do in polite society?"

She raised one eyebrow. "Polite society, huh? Where the hell have you been the last ten years? Because

the society I've seen over the last ten years is anything *but* polite."

"Touché." He stepped away from her and turned on
a lantern.

They were in the basement of the building, mostly
collapsed above them. A threadbare couch, a couple
of small tables, and an old cot stood against one wall.
A six-foot-high and probably three times as long
pile of rubble on the other end of the room was evidence that some of the building above now lived in
the basement below. For the ruins of an old building,
it was spruced up more than she'd expected.

Ridge tossed her a metal cup and pointed at one
of the barrels he'd lined up down the center of the
room. "Water is clean. Help yourself to a drink. You
may be here a while. Biff and Brandy will hunt for
you for a while. They are stupid, but persistent."

"Friends of yours?" she asked.

"I avoid the goon squad as much as you do, I'd imagine."

His green eyes continued to glow in the dim light as
they tracked her movements across the floor.

She guzzled a glass of water, watching him from the
corner of her eye. "Why are you avoiding them?"

He sat on the edge of the couch, his elbows resting on his knees. "I went AWOL. Not that we would ever get leave." He dropped his eyes, then raised them back up. "Were you trying to get their attention up there?"

As the blood rushed to her cheeks, she was thankful for the dim lighting to hide her blush. "No."

"Were you out here looking for them? Or me?"

Sure her cheeks were even redder, she turned, re-filling her cup. "I was making sure you left the trailer park and stayed away, yes. I was working my way back when I heard them." Her voice took on a far-away quality. "He was one of the ones who took me from the recruitment room, strapped me to the table. The ones who took me to those labs, over and over again."

She hadn't heard him move, but he was beside her with a comforting hand on her shoulder. It surprised her that her first instinct was to lean into him for support, not rear back and punch him.

Karma stepped away, shrugging off his hand. "What did you do for them?"

"You want me to answer your questions, but you won't even tell me your name?"

She wasn't used to feeling like prey. *He made her feel like prey.* The feeling exhilarated her more than it scared her. Each step she retreated, he advanced, until her back was against a concrete section of wall propped up by the rubble pile behind it.

"Nowhere else to run, pet."

That nickname, the one Pip always used, sent her blood boiling. Her fist shot out, but he caught it in his hand. He caught her other hand and blocked her knee, trapping her against the concrete wall with his body.

"You *really* don't like to be called pet, huh?" his voice practically purred. "Give me your name. I might use it instead." He shifted his head, nuzzling her neck. "You saved me, shared food with me. Now I've saved you, shared water with you."

The sensation of his face so close to her neck sent her blood racing, but not with fear. "So we're even." Her voice held a breathy quality she hadn't intended-ed.

"Nope. I've already given you my name."

She shoved him away, needing space as her temperature rose. "So I owe you mine?"

"It's only fair."

She could swear he was batting his eyes.

"I promise not to call you 'pet' again," he began. "Unless I'm trying to piss you off."

She rolled her eyes. "Yeah, I have a feeling if you continue to hang around me, pissed off will be a constant state."

"You came to me this time, pet."

"Karma! Geez, it's Karma. Like, if you don't stop calling me 'pet,' karma is going to come around and bite you in the ass!"

"Was that so hard?" he asked innocently, and she was *sure* he was batting his eyes now.

Suddenly, she was wrapped up in his arms again, pinned with her back to his chest, and his hand clamped over her mouth. She writhed and fought to get free.

"Shhh," he whispered right against her ear.

The sounds of footsteps finally registered. She froze in place, not daring to even breathe as the panic threatened to choke her again.

Ridge's hand against her stomach smoothed over her shirt, his thick arm encompassing her abdomen, pulling her tighter and coming to rest with his fingers on the flesh above her hip, playing with the skin between the hem of her shirt and the top of her jeans.

Her mind short-circuited. She sucked in a lungful of air, all of it spiced with his scent. His fingers were hot where they teased her cooler skin. She tensed against the need to press her body closer, to soak in the warmth radiating from him.

A stomp directly over the trap door she'd fallen through caused her to jump, and Ridge's grip to tighten almost painfully, bringing her mind back to the danger at hand. She dislodged herself from him, prepared to fight.

His claws unsheathed, the wickedly sharp black nails reflecting the dim light in the room.

The stomps repeated a few times before the footsteps retreated.

They remained still and alert for several minutes, waiting to see if someone would return.

Karma's blood pounded in her ears, adrenaline making her hands tremble.

Ridge was the first to relax. He brought her a cup of water, placed his hand on the small of her back, and led her to the couch, pressing her into it. "When did you escape?" His words were spoken so softly they almost didn't register with her.

"Three years, four months, and fourteen days from the day I arrived."

He nodded, his eyes unfocused. "I was there just shy of five years. They're under the impression I died."

"They have no such illusions about me." She gave him a wry smile. "I've made their lives miserable at every opportunity. Although, Biff seemed to think I was either dead or long gone."

He raised an eyebrow in her direction. "What exactly have you been doing to them?"

"As you saw, I'm often grocery shopping."

"You go in there regularly?"

"It depends," she evaded. "I started out raiding the supply trucks. They've put too many guards around and other security measures where the barges dock, so I avoid that part of the shore at all costs, now." Karma looked up at him. "What about you? What's your story?"

"I was part of the goon squad for a while after they completed my altering. I'm not proud of it. They trained me to fight. I was on the clean-up crew. Gather the person and bring them in. Handle them if they fought, but most were so doped up that they didn't know which way was up. My last job, I was sent to grab a badger who'd somehow gotten away.

The upper levels were adamant they get him back. He had kids. A slew of them. And he was all they had. I couldn't do it. I don't know where he got the blood, nor do I want to. We practically painted the walls with it. And I got him and his kids out. Took them to the river and watched until he had them out of sight."

"You didn't go with him?"

"No. I have penance to pay for what I did, what I helped do."

Karma nodded. She understood that completely.

"What else have you done besides grocery shopping? I know they can't be too mad about that, unless you are taking it by the truckload."

"I've been known to break people out of the labs before they get too far in the Altered process. If I can get to them quick enough, they are no worse for wear. If not," she shrugged, "I've lost a few who were too far to stop, but too early to be completed."

"What happened to them?"

"Some got sick and died. Some lost their minds and became a danger to others." Her mind drifted back to one of those cases. Lily's mom. "I learned quickly that they couldn't just be returned to their families. They would stay with me for weeks, sometimes months, depending on when I could get to them. I'm much more resilient than their kids." She closed her eyes against the memory of the scar running down Lily's back, but closing her eyes only made the image clearer. "If they were safe with me after a few months, not showing any signs of their animal, they could go home, or leave the area. If not, I dealt with it."

"You had to kill them." It wasn't a question.

"At least I did it humanely. It was better than any treatment they'd have gotten from Phoenix."

Chapter 6

5713

Karma

Ridge hadn't judged her for her actions, but that did nothing to assuage her guilt. The people she tried to help were just like her. They'd been desperate. They pushed away their worries, the rumors, and the unknown, telling themselves it would all be okay. Phoenix Corps would help them, provide for them, and their families would thrive. After all, who would stay at the big, clean, sturdy building on the edge of town if they were being mistreated?

They didn't realize the facility was a prison.

Standing in the hazy light, a few feet from the trap-door she'd fallen through, Karma swept her gaze from one spot to the next, making sure Biff and

Brandy were truly gone. Despite the water Ridge had given her, her throat felt raw from her earlier screams. Her hands were still unsteady from the residual adrenaline.

She turned to Ridge. "Thank you."

He gave her a slight nod, scanning the area as well.

In this light, she noticed a pallor to his skin, deep, dark circles under his haunting green eyes. She angled her body to face him, narrowing her focus to him. "How are you feeling?"

"Swell," he said sarcastically and rolled his eyes.

It was the rolling of his eyes that did it. He swayed with the motion.

Karma reached out a hand to steady him and felt the heat of his arm. He'd have seemed warm regardless since she was colder-blooded, but he shouldn't have *that* much higher a temperature, especially through the fabric of his shirt.

"Do you have medicine here?" she asked.

"No need. I'm fine," he insisted. The continued sways belied his statement.

She intended to move to his side, to steady him, and move him back down into his basement home.

But his eyes rolled back in his head and his knees buckled.

Karma caught the brunt of his weight before he hit the floor. "*I guess he's coming back with me... again.*"

She was careful in the route she took. Roundabout enough to disguise her scent for anyone looking to follow it, but short enough to get Ridge back to the trailers as fast as possible.

Shouldering her way back into the trailer, she lay Ridge back on the bed he had occupied the last time he'd been there. He was still unconscious, and his temperature seemed to be rising. She trotted to the other end and pushed open the door to the hidden hallway.

Lily stood there.

"Bring me a bucket of groundwater from the tunnels. The coldest you can find. Have Peter gather some dirt in another bucket and bring it to me. Also, grab me any of the medicines still left. I doubt if there's any that will be useful, but bring it anyway."

Lily rushed back down the hallway and into Mrs. Thorn's trailer.

Karma retraced her steps to the bedroom and checked Ridge's temperature again. His skin scorched hers. She set to work, pulling his arms out of his shirtsleeves and rolling him side to side to get the garments off him. As the skin of his arm was revealed, the stark lines of infection sharply contrasted with his pale skin.

He barely groaned as she moved him around, but his brow wrinkled in discomfort.

Lily stopped at the door, a bucket in each hand. "I left the last of the medicine I could find in the kitchen." She placed the buckets on the floor, then wrung her hands together. "Do you need me to help?"

Karma lifted her eyes from the grotesque appearance of his arm. "Dip a glass of water out of the bucket for now. Then, if you can bring me one more bucket of water, I'll use that to keep him hydrated." She hesitated for a moment. "Stay in the tunnels and leave via Mrs. Thorn's." Lily nodded and backed out of the room as she lifted Ridge's head, dripping water into his mouth until he swallowed.

They were a few months from winter, so no snow, and they didn't have much in the way of blankets and towels anymore, so mud would have to do. Karma cringed as she piled dirt around Ridge's neck, down the uninfected arm, and over his abdomen. They'd never get this old mattress clean again.

Using the bucket of water, she dampened the dirt to draw out some of the heat his fever was causing. Careful probing revealed a still-open and weeping wound on the top of his shoulder, near the base of his neck—probably the wound that nicked his artery. Karma recleaned the wound and added more water to the mud pack, as the heat from his body had dried it out already.

Once done, she went to the kitchen and sorted through the remaining medicines. They were all well past their expiration dates, but maybe one would still be good enough to help bring his fever down. And Lily, sweet girl, had left four cans of food on the counter for her and Ridge.

Throughout the rest of the day and long into the night, Karma stayed at his side, changing the mud pack and getting as much fluid into him as she could. His continued unconsciousness worried her. Late in the night, examining him by lantern, she noticed the spiderweb of infection around his shoulder had grown, protruding further up his neck and across his well-defined chest. The spread of infection wasn't the only worrisome thing. A small area of his wound continued to weep yellowish fluid and had yet to close over. His skin, hot to the touch still, blazed with heat the closer her hand to the oozing puncture.

She nearly slapped herself on the forehead. Stupid. She didn't think to check for fragments of Pip's teeth in his wounds. There hadn't been time when they were escaping from the building, and by the time she got him back to the trailer, she'd assumed his wounds were all closed. Karma jumped up and ran into the kitchen, searching for the first aid kit Lily had brought to her before.

Her hand brushed it, knocking it to the floor of the cabinet she'd shoved it in, spilling its contents. She grabbed the sharp scalpel she'd stolen from Phoenix Corps ages ago during one of her trips to visit, re-turning to his bedside.

Karma was about to touch the scalpel to Ridge's skin when she heard a familiar noise from the hallway.

"I heard you moving around up here. Is everything okay?"

"What did I say?" Karma asked.

"You might need help. I listened to make sure I wasn't hearing him move around."

"He's altered with some kind of big cat, Lil. If he didn't want you to hear him, you wouldn't."

"He's breathing fast."

Karma watched the rapid, shallow rise and fall of his chest. "He's really sick. I think there might be a piece of tooth lodged in one of his wounds."

"Your teeth?"

She shook her head. Karma started to lower the blade again, then stopped. "Bring me what is left of the rope I used to tie him to the bed earlier."

"I can help." Lily handed her the rope, standing too close to the bed for Karma's comfort.

"He's not like the others, I don't think," Karma said, "But I'm not sure. And I won't risk you." Karma raised her eyes to Lily. "He may wake fighting when I cut his wound back open. Go to the hall door and wait there. If things go bad, get to Rosie and Peter. Get them out and away from here." She raised her hand to stop Lily's protest. "Go."

Karma removed the mudpack from his uninjured arm and tied the rope around it, wrapping it around the bedframe and under, securing it to his feet again. She lacked confidence in the rope's ability to hold him, frayed as it was from the last time she'd used it.

Sitting back down next to him, Karma picked the scalpel up and returned to the task at hand.

At the first touch of the blade, blazing green eyes opened wide, and his mouth opened in a silent scream, arching his back off the bed, pulling the rope taut. A putrid smell wafted up from the wound as pus and fresh blood mixed and leaked through the now wide-open wound.

Those blazing eyes locked on hers. "One of the wounds you took from Pip is infected. I need you to lie as still as you can, so I can clean it out."

Pulling the black hairs of his fur out of the way, Karma pushed at the area around the wound until only blood remained. A low moan escaped his lips at the first hard push against his skin, white lines marring his face, indicating the strength he used to clamp his jaws closed. By the second, he'd drifted back into unconsciousness.

She dribbled clean water into the wound, blood swirling with the water and running down onto the abused mattress of the bed. Satisfied it was as clean as she could get it, Karma shined the lantern light into the opening. Deep within the wound, she found the offending shard of tooth. Without tweezers and her increased strength, she wouldn't have been able to pry the shard from where it was lodged in the bone of his shoulder.

Karma bandaged and wrapped the wound with her remaining supplies, then finally untied Ridge from the bed. She replaced the mud pack and crossed her fingers that he'd pull through. Moving like a zombie, she cleaned up as best she could, then made some of the dreaded dandelion coffee. She smiled at the collection of new roots she spotted under the kitchen window, left there to dry from Peter and Lily's foraging while she'd been out.

Coffee made, she trudged back in and sat on the floor next to the bed, exhaustion overwhelming her.

Chapter 7

7619

Ridge

Blinding pain pulled him from bliss.

Opening his mouth in a silent scream, his gaze connected with haunting gray eyes. These weren't the eyes of his torturers. She wore no lab coat, no scrubs, no mask. He read sorrow in those eyes, as if she felt bad for the pain.

The plump, pink lips belonging to his torturer moved, but he only heard "Wah, wah, wah."

Fire burned over his body, an inferno consuming him. But it was nothing compared to the pressure and stabbing pain. His vision narrowed, threatening to pull him back to the darkness, and he surrendered to it.

An overwhelming, itchy feeling brought him out of the darkness. His mouth, dry as the desert, demanded a drink. The dull light in the room indicated the sun was just beginning to peek over the horizon. An unfamiliar weight lay in his hand. Ridge twitched his fingers, trying to gauge what rested there.

He tried to turn his head, but the pain from the other side of his neck deterred the action. His head pounded. He ignored it. A mop of brownish-gray hair lay at the edge of his bed, and the weight in his hand was another hand. A female hand. He inhaled. He knew that scent—Karma. Her scent was clean with a spicy undertone, without floral or fruity adornments like the soaps used to hide scents at Phoenix Corps. He'd known that scent since their first encounter. He couldn't get enough of that scent into his lungs. It made him want to curl up with it.

Ridge looked up at the quiet gasp and saw the young, blonde girl in the doorway, the same one he'd stolen rats from in the grocery store.

He tried to sit up, but broke out in a cold sweat with the pain and effort of the movement.

The girl rushed forward, only to be shoved back out of the room in a flash of movement he'd barely seen.

"Out. I told you to stay away from here." Karma's voice vibrated with rage as she blocked the girl's body from his view.

"I was worried. I hadn't heard any movement. I thought something had happened to you." The girl's quiet voice held unshed tears.

Karma's tone quieted, softer than before, all trace of rage gone. "All the more reason for you to stay away." Karma sighed. "Go. We're fine here."

The girl's footsteps were so light, he'd not have heard them if he hadn't been paying close attention, or the strange scraping sound on the other end of the trailer, before the only sound left was the sound of Karma breathing.

She turned those haunting grey eyes to him.

He felt her gaze like a physical touch.

Karma stepped closer to the bed and laid her hand on his forehead, neck, then shoulder. "Your fever is down." She made her way to the other side of the bed and leaned down, examining his other shoulder.

The touch of her fingers whispered over the skin, sending sparks over his nerve endings. The fur of his panther stuck through the ragged edges of his human skin. Her touch pushed the hair against the grain and raised goosebumps over his flesh. "The last wound is closed. It was festering, causing the infection. Part of one of Pip's teeth was lodged in the bone."

His voice scratchy from dryness, he asked, "And the mud?" It was the cause of the itchiness crawling over his arm and chest.

"A mud pack to cool you down. Your fever was really high." She dipped a can into a bucket and lifted it to him.

His hand shook as he reached to take it from her.

She pulled it away from his shaking hand. "I can help."

Up to that moment, he'd not have thought her shy, but a slight blush rose to her pale cheeks as she helped to prop him up, then held the glass while he took the prescribed "small sips" she continually instructed.

His eyes were threatening to slam shut when she guided him back flat onto the mattress, and his whole body shook with the effort he'd exerted, which hadn't been much, since she'd done most of the work.

"Rest."

He shook his head. "I need to go. I need to clean up and go." His voice betrayed his weakness.

She didn't need to put in any effort as she laid her hand on his cheek. Just the weight of her hand held him still. "Rest for now. You can go soon."

His eyes slammed shut, and he didn't have the strength to open them again.

Chapter 8

5713

Karma

She closed her eyes and leaned against the door frame of the bedroom. Her deep inhale brought nothing but his scent. He'd been close to death: the raging fever, the rapidly spreading infection. The thoughts gripped her, a vise squeezing her heart, bringing tears to her eyes, and making it hard to breathe. No one deserved to die at the hands of Phoenix Corp, but losing Ridge—she didn't want to examine why that thought threatened to bring her to her knees.

She barely knew the guy.

Karma shook her head to clear those thoughts and grabbed the bucket. She headed down to the water barrels they kept stored underground. Peter, Rosie, and Lily sat on the threadbare couch, continuing to weave bedrolls and blankets from the plastic bags they'd been gathering.

She quietly walked to the barrel and dipped the bucket to collect more clean water.

Lily stood next to her when she turned to head back. "I'm sorry." Shame laced her tone.

"I'm sorry, too," Karma replied. "I shouldn't have snapped at you. I appreciate your concern for me. But, he's Altered, Lily. You've already tangled with him once and experienced how much stronger, faster, and more cunning he is. I don't know him well enough to believe you are safe with him. Any of you." She swung her gaze, taking in Rosie and Peter still sitting on the couch, watching their interaction, rather than weaving now. "Keeping you three and this community safe is my first priority. Keeping you hidden is the best way for me to do that with him here. Once he returns to where he came from, you are welcome to move around as usual. But for now, *please*, do as I ask and stay down here."

Receiving nods from each of them, Karma grabbed her bucket and started out of the room.

"If he's not safe, what about you?" Lily asked quietly to her back.

Karma set the bucket down and turned to face Lily, wrapping her in an embrace. "He's weak as a kitten right now. He helped me against Pip. It's how he ended up in this predicament. Once he's feeling better, he'll go back to where he came from. Thank you for worrying about me, but I'm better equipped to handle him, and the less he knows about us, the better."

Lily nodded.

"You're still good on food down here for now, right?" Karma looked from Lily to Peter and back.

"Lily said she would go check the traps later today. We are good on our supplies, though," Peter replied.

"Lil, stay within the trailer park boundaries. You can check the traps we've set here. I don't want you venturing out without me right now. The last visit to Phoenix Corps stirred up a hornet's nest. They have the goon squad out in force looking for me."

"But..."

"No," Karma interrupted. "I'll go out myself and check the other traps soon. Within the trailer park. Promise me, Lil."

Reluctantly, Lily nodded.

"This isn't like the instructions to stay out of my trailer while Ridge is here. You can't ignore this."

"Fine." Her petulant tone almost made Karma smile. Lily had lost the ability to be a child long before. Forced to grow up too fast, Karma always hated that for her. The moments of rebellion were a welcome sight, even if they were potentially dangerous.

"Stay safe. Stay quiet." Karma lifted the bucket and made her way back up to her trailer.

Karma left the bucket in the kitchen and stepped away from the sound of his soft snores. The air outside held a chill, but the rising sun showed promise of some warmth.

She moved to the edge of the trailer park, past burnt shells and rotting structures. No unusual scents caught her nose as she wound her way around the area. Only ten of the trailers were livable. She'd managed to position them, thanks to her increased strength and some help from the other residents, to hide the ones that were still inhabitable.

Jacob Lowry sat on his porch as she came around the corner to his place. He waved a gnarled hand, his usual gesture of shooing her away.

Further along in the process than a lot of the people she pulled from Phoenix Corps, Jacob had been in the reject pile. Their experiments hadn't gone as planned. The animal they'd tried to splice him with, some sort of bird, crippled his dominant hand. His fingers were bent at odd angles, and it appeared his wrist had been repeatedly broken.

He didn't bother to acknowledge the two cans of food she'd placed on the porch near his feet. He hated relying on her for help. Her offers to help him leave the area went ignored.

She nodded at him, waved goodbye, and kept walking.

Next, she knocked on the door of Annabeth's trailer, tucked into a small alcove on the edge of the property. It sure looked in rough shape on the exterior. The aluminum siding on one side was rusted through. Karma had scavenged supplies to help her seal the trailer from the inside. Annabeth was young, not much older than Lily.

She'd come to the trailer park when Karma pulled her father, Elliot, from the hands of Phoenix Corps.

A month had passed, and she thought he was in the clear. She'd been very wrong.

Karma found Annabeth unconscious on the porch, a gash and lump on her head.

Elliot screamed into the void and threw anything that wasn't nailed down. He went back at Annabeth again. Karma stopped him.

When Annabeth regained consciousness, Karma had to tell her that her father was gone. She'd been inconsolable.

Karma handed Annabeth a couple of cans.

"Thank you," Annabeth said.

"Do you need anything else? Other supplies running low?"

"I'm good. How is Lily? I haven't seen her for a couple of days."

"Lily is good. She will check the traps later and can bring you some of the catch, if she's found any."

"That would be great."

Karma nodded and backed off the small porch attached to the front, careful of the rotten boards.

Lily could sometimes coax Annabeth into talking a bit, and they had a tentative friendship. But Annabeth was usually pretty shy around Karma.

She dropped another can at the next trailer.

Karma had gotten Judy out before she'd gotten far enough to get any traits of the brown bear they'd attempted to splice her with. Once the treatments started, they had to be given at specific intervals. If the intervals were interrupted in any way, the body would reject further attempts, and they couldn't be restarted.

A lot of the people Karma had gotten out as early as Judy had asked her to help them get away from Fairway. But Judy wanted to stay.

She'd check on a few of the others later, but for now, Karma headed back to her trailer and the patient inside.

Entering the bedroom, Ridge's soft snores reached her ears. She placed the bucket on the floor next to the bed, grabbed a couple of rags from the kitchen, and knelt next to the bed. She brushed away the dried dirt from his muscular body, encouraged by the fact that the furious streaks of infection across his chest were receding. Once the worst of the dirt was gone, Karma took a dampened rag and gently cleaned his skin.

Now that his sickness had passed, she couldn't help but notice the softness of his skin and the contrasting hardness of the muscles beneath.

He moaned at her touch with the wet rag, his hand striking out with lightning speed, capturing her wrist in the vise of his grip. His eyes flew open, the neon green locking with hers.

Her heart raced, and her breath caught. She didn't pull away, though in his weakened state, she could've broken his hold. Karma reached forward and laid her free hand on his chest, giving a slight push as he attempted to lift his body into a sitting position. "You're safe. Rest and heal. I'll get you clean of the mud and dirt, then I'll bring you some food."

He tightened his fingers around her wrist and narrowed his eyes suspiciously. They slammed shut in the next moment, and his grip went lax. His breathing evened out once again as he drifted back into the healing sleep.

Karma took a deep, steadying breath and continued her ministrations.

His breathing remained even as she finished. She cleaned up the mess she'd made and went to the kitchen to prepare some food. Lily had brought up more cans of hearty soups. They'd be easy for him to chew, but still contained a good amount of meat, which he would need to regain his strength.

The food was almost ready when he started screaming.

Karma shoved the pot away from the heat and ran into the bedroom.

Ridge still slept but thrashed violently in the bed. His good arm swung erratically, and his feet kicked out.

She was frozen by the sight, torn between her safety and his terror. Her heart squeezed uncomfortably. Karma remembered the terrors she endured after being taken by Phoenix Corp, the terrors that still gripped her even now.

Karma stepped into the room and caught his arm by the wrist as it flailed.

Ridge's hand twisted, grasping her forearm in return, and yanked her down to him. Chest to chest, his legs wrapped around to pin her legs beneath.

"Shh, you're safe, Ridge." She kept her voice light, refusing to give in to the fear. Even in his weakened state, she was thoroughly pinned and at his mercy.

His chest heaved with great, gasping breaths, and the vise of his arm tightened painfully across her back and ribs. His eyes were open, but unseeing. The bright green orbs stared right through her.

Sweat beaded on his forehead, and she could feel the heat of him along her length. She wanted to curl up against him and absorb the radiating heat. His steady warmth, she knew instinctively, would be better than the few times she'd been able to bask in the weakened sunlight when it finally made its way through the dust and debris in the atmosphere.

Despite his weakness, in the blink of an eye, he'd reversed their positions, pinning her to the bed beneath him. The contrast of the cool, damp mattress against her back and the heat of his body along her front sent her nerves into overdrive. The hand that had banded around her back was free and wrapped around her throat.

Karma tightened the muscles of her neck, fighting his punishing grip, refusing to give in to the crushing pressure he used. "Ridge," she whispered. "You're safe here with me, Ridge."

He blinked once, twice, and then his vision cleared, sharpened on her, and his grip relaxed. He closed his eyes, blowing out a harsh breath. His hand cupped her jaw, thumb gliding over her cheek, coming to rest at the corner of her mouth. "I'm sorry." The words whispered over her face, barely loud enough to hear.

"I'm okay. It was only a nightmare." Her voice shook, but not with fear. Awareness of him amplified. Every place he touched, her nerves sparked, waves of lightning webbing over her nerve endings and beyond.

His mouth crashed into hers, a searing kiss intensifying her already overstimulated nerves. Crushed together as they were, his growing length along her thigh was vividly apparent.

She gasped as his lips trailed down her neck, nipping and sucking at the sensitive flesh.

His hand roamed over her chest, pulling her shirt up, caressing her bare skin.

Karma barely noticed the tremble ripple through his body at first, so caught up in the sensations of his hand and lips. The second time, it registered, and his body collapsed on hers, his injured arm giving out.

He let out a harsh, frustrated grunt, and he clenched his jaw.

She carefully wiggled out from underneath him and helped him roll on his back.

Ridge's skin had grown cold and clammy.

Noticing the marked pallor of his skin, Karma laid her hand against his forehead.

He was warm, but not feverish.

"I'll bring you something to eat. It should help you get your strength back." She quickly retreated from the room.

Back in the kitchen, she dunked a hand in the cool, clear water of the bucket and pressed a hand to her flaming cheek. Things had gotten quickly out of hand. Not since Dorian...

She'd long ago stopped waiting for his return, stopped wearing his ring. It was the one thing she refused to sell to get money for food after the quake, after he left, before she'd gone to Phoenix for help.

She shook her head to clear it and spooned some of the soup into a can. Karma pulled the band from her ponytail, letting her hair drape over her face, hiding her flaming cheeks from view. Carrying the can into the bedroom, she set it beside the bed and spoke without looking at him. "Let me help you sit up, so you can eat. I'll come back and get the can when you're done."

Karma arranged herself behind him and lifted, mindful of his shoulder. Scooting him back, so he rested against the trailer wall, she moved out of the way and handed him the can of warm soup.

Ridge's hand shot out, catching her wrist. "Karma..."

"I need to finish cleaning up. I'll be back in a bit." She still refused to look at him.

His audible sigh tugged at her heart, but he let her go.

Chapter 9

Ridge

Karma had made herself scarce the rest of the day. She brought him meals and water, but beyond that, Ridge had no idea where she'd been most of the day. There hadn't been any sign of the young blonde either.

He must have been close to death. Despite the sleep he'd gotten, he still felt weak, and exhaustion pulled at him, especially when he tried to move on his own.

Karma made sure that every time she came in to help him move, she touched him as little as possible. But it didn't matter. He was drawn to her.

His instinct was to protect her, had been since he'd seen her the first time. He'd step between her and Pip again to protect her. Ridge didn't have to deal much with Pip when he was at Phoenix Corps, but he was familiar with the shark's reputation. They'd picked an appropriate animal when they spliced him.

The opening of the main door alerted him to her return. When she poked her head into the room, her hair was still down, a curtain hiding her face from view. He managed to get himself to a sitting position, but frustration grated on his nerves with how weak and tired he felt with just that small movement.

"Ready for something more to eat?" she asked quietly.

He gave a small nod. His eyes were drawn to her retreating figure, admiring her curves and the sway of her hips as she walked away. The sounds of clanging pots and pans had him picturing her out there, wishing he could see her, watch her graceful and sure movements. Soon, the smell of roasting meat filtered into the room, and his stomach made itself known with a deep growl.

"Won't be long," Karma called in to him from the kitchen.

He must have dozed off for a moment. The tinkling of the can being set on the table next to the bed brought him instantly awake. His hand shot out, capturing Karma's wrist before she could scuttle away. His eyes met her haunting gray ones. He read wariness there.

Her eyes dropped pointedly to where his gripped her.

"Stay?" His voice was tentative, hopeful.

Karma's head dipped in the slightest affirmation, and he released her. She turned away and brought in her own can of food, then grabbed the chair she'd sat on while attending to him and dragged it as close to the doorway as possible.

He did his best to hide his grin behind the can as he scooped up the meat and broth. The soup tasted like it came from a can, slightly metallic and bland, but it was hot and hit the spot.

They ate in silence, and Karma stared at the can in her hand like it held the answers to all the world's problems.

Placing his empty can back on the table, he scooted down, feeling his eyes growing heavy. "The blonde. Where is she?"

Karma's demeanor changed. Her posture stiffened further, and if she'd been a porcupine, her quills would be standing on end.

"She's safe." Her curt tone left no question that the topic was closed to any further discussion. She scooped up his can and left the room. "Rest, so you can regain your strength and go back home."

Even as darkness pulled him under, he grinned.

He'd go back home, but he wouldn't stay away.

Chapter 10

5713

Karma

Karma set the cans in the sink. She needed to haul some water upstairs to use for washing, but first, her hands needed to stop shaking.

He was a stranger—an Altered stranger at that. When he reached out to her, simply the feel of his hand on her wrist made her blood race. He'd not ventured beyond the bedroom and main entrance of her trailer, yet his scent permeated every surface. She'd even washed up and changed clothes while he slept and still...

His soft snores drifted from the room.

Karma tiptoed to the doorway, careful to avoid the three floorboards that creaked, and peeked around the door frame.

She took in the softness of his face, contrasting the sculpted muscles of his torso and arms—she nearly sighed at the memory of being in those strong arms. She wasn't in charge there. She didn't *have* to be.

His sharp, green eyes opened, staring into hers.

The intensity of his gaze hit her like a physical blow. She gasped and backpedaled out of the room, heat rising on her cheeks. Her hip crashed hard into the corner of the kitchen counter, eliciting a yelp from her. Karma clamped a hand over her mouth to stifle the sound, but heard him trying to move from the bed. "I'm fine. Say there and rest," she said quickly, her voice higher in pitch and more rushed than she intended.

His soft chuckle had her racing out the door.

Slamming the door shut behind her, she drew in the air outside, but still it tasted tainted with his scent. She couldn't escape it.

Karma dropped hard to the steps leading into the trailer, worrying her hands together, unsure if she could separate the longing from the despair.

Before now, she'd never even looked at someone other than Dorian. They'd been together since they were in school. He'd been gone for over nine years now. Dorian wouldn't be back, and she'd never see the body.

But why did she feel such an overwhelming sense of guilt? And the terror of "what ifs" when it came to who and what Ridge was. Her heart screamed that she could trust him—he'd come to her rescue with Pip, with the goon squad. But the little voice in her head whispered the potential dangers.

He was altered. They would, at least, be matched in a fight. She couldn't guarantee a win for her.

He was a product of Phoenix Corps. Phoenix didn't like to lose. They'd recapture her if they could. And, sending in a spy to make her vulnerable— she wouldn't put it past them.

Ridge nearly died from the infection. His current weakness attested to just how close he came. The thready pulse she'd barely felt during the worst of his illness—the vise gripping her heart tightened again at the thought of losing him.

A thud from inside had her on her feet and racing into the trailer.

Ridge lay inside the kitchen, face down on the worn linoleum floor.

Karma slid across the floor to her knees. When she turned him over, those mesmerizing green eyes stared back.

A half-grimace, half-smile slid over his face. "Not ready to walk on my own yet, I guess."

She blew out a frustrated breath. "Ya think? How much damage did you do?"

"I just got dizzy. I don't think I hurt anything further with the fall."

"Remind me not to leave you unsupervised."

His answering smirk brought heat to her cheeks.

She tried but suspected she failed to sound disgusted. "Not volunteering myself here."

Karma helped him to his feet and back to bed. She carried more of his weight than she expected to need to, and he huffed and puffed with the effort he used.

Once he settled back into bed, she asked, "What were you getting up for?"

"Water. And I was going to come find you."

"I'll bring you more water and some more food. I'll run out and grab some from the supplies we have. You are going to need more than you've had so far to regain your strength, it seems."

He grabbed her wrist when she stood.

She looked from his hand to his eyes. There was a question there, a pleading that she didn't want to answer. "I'll only be gone a few minutes." She lightened her tone a bit. "You can be trusted for a few minutes to stay put, right? Or do I need to break out the rope again?"

"Good luck getting the rope to hold me again."

"I just picked your ass up off the floor. I suspect even the length of frayed rope I have left would do the trick if I needed."

His tone shifted from playful to serious. "You can trust me, Karma."

Chapter 11

5713

Karma

You can trust me, Karma.

The words echoed in her head.

She made her way into the underground tunnel and greeted Peter and Rosie, sitting on the couch, weaving away. Lily wasn't anywhere to be seen.

"Lily is checking the traps," Peter answered before Karma could voice the question.

She nodded and filled another bucket with water. She grabbed a few more cans with high protein content, shoving them in a bag to carry them more easily. "If she gets any fresh meat, have her bring me some, please. She can bring it through the *outside* door, not the hallway."

Rosie and Peter both nodded.

"How is the altered?" Rosie asked.

"Stubborn. If he doesn't rest, he may never get well enough to leave."

Rosie's brow rose at something she heard in Karma's tone. "Is that a bad thing?"

"Yes." Even Karma heard the doubt in her tone then. She spun on her heel and headed back the way she came.

She made sure Ridge ate several servings of the canned food she brought from their supply and kept his water full, hoping that it would keep him in bed. He dozed between meals, and she kept herself busy weaving in the kitchen area, so she was close by if he decided to go for another walk.

With each meal, he was a bit stronger, the healing kicking in.

It had grown dark outside, with no visit from Lily, so Karma figured the traps within the park were all empty.

She was just dozing off herself on the cramped and uncomfortable bench seat masquerading as a couch in the living room of the trailer when a frantic knock sounded at the door.

Peter stood on the other side, terror written on his face.

"What's..." she didn't get to finish.

"Lil isn't back."

"What do you mean?"

"She hasn't come back. She went out to check the traps, like you said, but she didn't come back."

"She was supposed to stay in the park."

Peter kicked at the dirt with the toe of his worn sneaker.

"Peter, did she tell you where she was going?"

Peter seemed to shrink at the question, appearing younger than his years.

Karma stooped to his level, which wasn't much smaller than her own height. "I can't find her if I don't know where to look, Peter. Please, tell me what you know. I won't be mad at you."

"The traps here are empty. She was going to check back at the grocery store and those on the way there and back."

She swallowed her frustration and anger, knowing it would still upset Peter, even if it wasn't directed at him. "Thank you."

Indecision wracked her. Peter was too young. Rosie was older, more frail, and if she was being honest with herself, Rosie was sick. The others in the trailer park stayed to themselves. They weren't interested in helping others. She didn't know how long she'd be gone. Or if she'd need to go to Phoenix Corps. She *always* made sure Lily stayed close if she had to go there, in case she didn't return.

Ridge cleared his throat. He stood at the doorway to the bedroom, leaning less heavily on it than he would have a few hours before.

Her gut told her she could trust him. And she really had no other choice. "This is Peter. He, Lily, and Rosie live here with me."

Ridge surveyed the trailer. "Where?"

"Peter can show you, when you are steady enough to not fall unless you are leaning on a wall."

He pushed off the wall and stood straight with only a small sway to him.

"I'm trusting you with them. I need to find Lily."

"Alone?"

"You're in no condition to be a knight in shining armor this time."

He cocked his eyebrow, and a rakish grin appeared. "Knight in shining armor, eh?"

She ignored the flutter in her belly. "Keep them safe?"

Ridge stepped forward and rested his hand along her cheek. "I will."

His thumb glided over her cheek. She fought off the need to lean into him, lean on his strength, his green eyes soft with sympathy and a longing she did her best to ignore.

Karma stepped away, her body stiffening with resolve. It was up to her to find Lily. She didn't need or want to lean on him. Turning on her heel, she walked out the door, letting it slam behind her.

She gulped in the rapidly cooling air of the evening, trying to fend off the overwhelming anxiety threatening her. "Damnit, Lily! Why didn't you listen?"

Karma sprinted into the dark toward the grocery store where they'd first encountered Ridge.

Karma followed the trail of Lily's scent through the back way they usually took to the defunct store. Her scent was interwoven with another familiar scent, but she ignored it, focusing only on Lily. Like Peter said, she had stopped at each of the traps on the way. One of the traps closest to the old store had fresh smells on it, but the rest had been empty. As she got closer to the storefront, Lily's scent grew weaker. When she veered off to follow the stronger scent, it became muddled with the scent of others.

Biff and Brandy.

Shit.

Keeping her pace steady to follow the scents, Karma wove through the streets, her heart in her throat. If Lily was in the hands of Biff and Brandy, she was in deep trouble. The idea of confronting Biff chilled her to the bone, but she would do whatever it took to get Lily back.

Using the darkness for cover, Karma split away from the scents and took a shorter path that would dump her out on the main road used by the service trucks.

As she approached the park boundary, she could smell the nocturnal animals out looking for their food. She ducked into the tree line and increased her speed again. Exhaust fumes started to overpower the scents of nature the closer she got to the road. The vibrations in the ground told her trucks were passing, even though she wasn't close enough to hear them.

Finally, the road came into view. Karma pressed against a tree trunk, squinting to peer into the darkness. She arrived as the tail end of a truck rode by. The face reflected in the side mirror sent a chill down her spine. The beady black eyes were unmistakable. Biff.

Karma ground her teeth. She hadn't seen any evidence of Lily in the truck, but she'd only caught a quick glimpse. It was unlikely Lily could've gotten away from Biff on her own, and Biff wasn't alone.

If they had Lily, they wouldn't hesitate to take her to the labs.

On the off-chance Lily got away, she'd head back to the trailer. Karma had to believe that Ridge would keep her and the others safe until Karma could return. Decision made, Karma dove back into the woods and headed for the broken fence line.

She scurried through the hole, following the path she'd taken countless times into the facility. There were more guards stationed at the truck entrance. Two faced the building while two others checked the oncoming vehicles. That was going to complicate matters.

Staying hidden in the shadows, Karma looked across the property. Nothing else changed there. The grassy lawn had no cover for her. She retreated and crept back through the break in the fence.

Following the fence line, she emerged from the park and kept going. This was an area of town even *she* avoided. Rot and refuse permeated the air, blocking out any useful smells. Broken glass littered every surface. Graffiti tagged any remaining walls. The people inhabiting this section of town—not even Phoenix Corps wanted them.

She moved as quickly as she could, jumping at the smallest of sounds. By the time she cleared the area, sweat rolled down her back.

The Phoenix Corp compound's size could be compared to a small town. She was winded and tired, and she'd only managed to make it to the corner of the property. She knew of another break in the fencing there and headed straight for it. Once through, Karma army crawled on the ground about a hundred yards, heaved open a manhole cover, and dropped down, pulling the cover back into place before trudging through the sewer system.

Karma pulled her shirt collar up over her nose in a futile effort to save her sense of smell. Sticking to the edges of the tunnels, she followed the path. Rodents scurried away from her, and she was forced to crouch when the tunnels narrowed.

The last space she crawled through had a maintenance hatch at the top. Pushing with all her might, she managed to move the lid and the pile of boxes stacked on it to the side and climbed through. She stripped off her ruined clothes and dropped them back down the hole, replacing the lid. The utility room she stood inside had overalls hanging on hooks next to the pipes running from this room to others in the facility. She quickly donned a set and found a pair of work boots among the bunch that were only a few sizes too big. She yanked a handkerchief from the pocket of one of the larger sets of overalls, and, hoping no one used it to blow their nose, she tied her hair up in it.

She cracked open the door and peered into the hallway.

The coast was clear.

Keeping her head down, she slipped out of the room and did her best to keep her face hidden from the cameras lining the route. She was three levels below the loading docks here. There were a few labs on this level, so she headed to those first.

She passed a few people in lab coats, but they were more focused on their clipboards than a lowly maintenance worker.

Karma peeked into the first lab she passed. The skinny window at the door didn't let her see much, but the person on the table had short, dark hair. Lily wasn't in there.

Hurrying further down, the next lab was empty. A man's screams echoed down the hallway from the final lab on this wing of the floor. Karma sped up in that direction. The screams had died to whimpers by the time she reached the door. She itched to find a way in to help the sandy-haired man strapped to the table. But if she helped him now, she'd never get to Lily.

Shouldering her way into the stairwell, she ambled leisurely down the stairs, wanting to draw as little attention to herself as possible.

Halfway down the stairs, the ground shook and the lights flickered. The continued aftershocks were now few and far between, but this one had perfect timing. She leapt the last section of stairs and pushed down the locked handle of the door to the next floor. Karma felt the mechanism inside the handle break and drove her weight into the door. It swung open, and she meandered down the next hall as it fell back into place.

Furious activity in the hall allowed her to pick up her pace.

The lab techs were running from room to room, checking on the victims inside and the electronic processes they used to inflict their torture. They paid no attention to Karma as she weaved through the halls as quickly as she dared, peering into room after room.

There were two labs left on this level. The first was dark. In the other room, another man's screams echoed out to her.

When she came in during other trips, the people she'd pulled out of the labs had been here for days or weeks, sometimes. But she remembered them putting her in these labs for the first time. She'd screamed and screamed. They'd left her in there, in the dark, for what felt like hours.

Karma crossed to the darkened lab door and watched the light of the badge scanner blink erratically. It was still down. Giving the lab door the same treatment as the stairwell door, she broke the lock and slid in.

Very little light from the hall filtered in, so her eyes were useless. Her hearing wasn't much better, but in here she could smell terror, and Lily.

"Lil."

A whimper was the only response.

Going by memory, Karma headed to where the table should be. Her hand bumped a tray, sending it clattering to the ground and eliciting a terrified but muffled scream from Lily.

"Shh, it's me, Lil."

Karma found the binding at Lily's wrist and yanked it free from the metal table. Skirting the table, she repeated the action on the other side, then moved to her feet. Those clamps were made of metal and were much harder to break. Karma blindly searched the tools she overturned, nicking her finger on one of the scalpels. When her hand landed on a thick pair of tweezers, she grabbed them and went to the foot of the table, where Lily scraped at her ankles with her nails.

She placed her hands over Lily's. "I'll get you free, Lil. Don't hurt yourself." Karma did her best to keep the urgency and stress from her voice.

Karma jammed the end of the tweezers into the hinge of the clamps holding Lily's feet to the table and pushed. The metal groaned as the pieces of the hinge gave way.

As soon as there was enough space, Lily pulled her feet free.

They'd taken her shoes.

As Karma guided her closer to the door, Lily pulled at a gag that had been too tight on her mouth, and blood ran from the corners of her lips, where it cut her. Quickly finding the scalpel, Karma cut the gag. A hunk of her hair fell to the floor.

Anger blazed hot through her blood, eclipsing Karma's relief in finding Lily.

Lily whimpered again. "I'm so sorry I didn't listen."

"Shh." She placed a gentle hand on Lily's shoulder. "Let's get you out of here. Okay? Then we'll discuss *why* I give you the rules I do."

Lily nodded, squeezing her eyes shut for only a second. When she opened them again, even in the dim light, Karma saw the shift. Determination bled from her every pore. Lily's posture changed, taking up the defensive stance they'd practiced so often.

Karma turned back to the door, but Lily's hand on her shoulder halted her movement.

"I knew you'd be mad, but I wanted to find meat for everyone. I passed Annabeth while checking the traps. She wanted to come with me."

She squeezed Lily's hand. "Let's get you out first. I'll help Annabeth next."

A lot of activity buzzed in the halls. Karma peered out the narrow window in the door, waiting for a break in the activity.

She pulled Lily in front of her. "Put your arms behind your back as if you're handcuffed. Hopefully, they'll just think I'm moving you to another room."

Lily did as she asked, and Karma pushed on the door with her shoulder. They slipped into the hallway, walking nonchalantly back toward the stairwell.

Karma heard the distinctive stomps of the goon squad. Finding it difficult to draw a deep breath with the pressure in her chest, she fought back the panic. She would get Lily out of here. They would waltz right out of here with no one the wiser. Those thoughts repeated through her head as she navigated through the people in lab coats coming and going around them.

She slipped down the hallway leading away from the stairwell, thankful she was as familiar with this layout as the people who lived and worked in this place. Three doors down, she shoved her way into yet another stairwell. "There are cameras in here as well. Keep your head down and your arms behind you," she mumbled.

On the next floor up, Karma broke the door locking mechanism again, thankful as the lights continued to flicker in the hallway and on the security pin pads at each door. Less activity in this hallway allowed her to breathe easier. They strolled into the hallway, past the other stairwell and labs, until they reached the maintenance room Karma had entered from.

Voices inside. Shit. They were in there trying to fix the systems that the aftershock knocked out. There were several other exit points Karma used over the years, but none were anywhere near this area. And, if the now steady lights from the furthest hallway were any indication, they'd have the security systems back in place soon. Double shit.

Salt water.

The stench hit her nose, and her grip tightened painfully on Lily's arm. Lily stifled a groan. Immediately, Karma relaxed her grip and increased her speed.

Pip barked orders at the goon squad down the next hallway.

Karma chose the storage room five doors down from the maintenance room. She shoved Lily inside and closed the door silently behind them.

"Be as still, calm, and quiet as you can. Pip is in the hall somewhere. He can feel heartbeats with his ugly face," she whispered. Karma turned, searching the shelves. She found a box with new scrubs and tossed a set to Lily. "Put these on."

The mechanic's jumpsuit she put on was close enough to the goon squad attire, so it wasn't strange to see her with Lily in the hospital gown. The goon squad rarely interacted with anyone in scrubs or lab coats. It might draw more attention, but it would cover Lily better.

"Did you hear the voices of the people in the mechanical room back there?" Karma asked quietly.

Lily nodded.

"Will you recognize them?"

Another nod.

"Let me know when you hear them talking in the hall. We need to get in that room, but not while they are in there."

Chapter 12

Karma

What seemed like hours later, Lily pointed at the door. "Out there," she mouthed. She listened for another minute and pointed down the hall away from the maintenance room. "They went that way."

Karma cracked the door and peeked out. No one was within sight, but she could smell the scents of a dozen different people, probably all still in the hallway somewhere. Looking like she belonged there had been the key to not being discovered in the past, so she pushed open the door confidently, guided Lily in front of her, and started down the hall.

Lily's hand was on the door to the mechanical room when chaos broke out.

"Five-Seven-One-Three! Pet, you *bitch*! Stop her!" Pip's voice, garbled because of the extra rows of teeth he had to talk around, rang out down the hall.

She didn't bother to look behind her. Karma shoved Lily into the room and slammed the door shut behind her. She grabbed a shelf, tearing it off its supports, and used it to wedge the door closed.

Lily's eyes were wide with fear, the whites visible all around her brown eyes.

Karma placed her hands on Lily's shoulders. "When you get into the tunnel, crawl fast until you can stand. Then run. You're going to go at least a mile, then start looking above. There will be an exit hatch. The lid is heavy. It's going to take all your strength to move it, but I know you can do it. You'll come out on Finley Avenue. Don't stop for anyone, don't look at anyone. Run. Run as far and as fast as you can. Ridge is at the trailer with Rosie and Peter. Get to them, get cleaned up, and stay safe."

"What about you?" Lily asked. "You aren't coming too?"

"The shelf won't hold forever. I don't want them following you into the tunnel. I'm going to get you in and cover the entrance. I'll meet you at home as soon as I can."

"They'll catch you!" she argued.

"Maybe. But I've escaped before. I'll do it again." When Lily opened her mouth to argue again, Karma raised her hand. "Rosie and Peter need someone to keep them safe. I trust you to keep them safe until I get home."

"Come with me!"

"I'll be close behind. I don't plan to surrender."

The shelf screamed in protest as they tried to break through the door.

"Go."

As soon as Lily was in the sewage tunnel, Karma replaced the lid and hid it back under the pile of boxes. Then she turned, looking for anything she could use as a weapon. One of the maintenance workers left their utility knife behind. It wasn't much, but it was better than nothing. She extended the blade as the shelf groaned and buckled, allowing the door to open a crack.

The brighter light from the hallway filtered in and bounced off an object, catching her attention. An eighteen-inch cast-iron pipe wrench winked at her in the stream of light. She tucked the utility knife in the pocket of her stolen coveralls and dove for the wrench as the door blasted open with enough force to put the handle through the concrete block wall it hit.

Like a professional baseball player, Karma swung the wrench at the first guy through the door. It wasn't Biff, but it might as well have been his twin. The impact sent him careening back into the group trying to get through the door. He wasn't getting back up.

She let the momentum of the swing spin her in a circle, adjusted her stance, and reentered the fray.

Pip's stench still permeated the air, and she heard his grating voice barking orders. "Pet, you and I have unfinished business. Don't think you are walking out of here today!"

Karma swung the wrench, knocking back one guy, then the next. Using it as a battering ram, she shoved it into an Altered's gut, shoving him back through the doorway and into the people behind him. Her speed left them no time to react, bowling them over into a pile.

She spun, intending to race down the hall, when Pip's greasy hand grabbed her hair. Screaming in frustration again, she spun, jamming the mouth of the wrench into Pip's horribly gaping maw. Several of his triangular teeth exploded from his mouth, blood gushing. She twisted the wrench, catching its teeth on Pip's lower teeth, and ripped outward, bringing more of his teeth with it. She whirled around, extending the utility knife, slicing it across his cheek, opening a deep gash in his human skin, the blade bouncing off the denticles underneath. A final crack with the wrench, and she sprinted down the hallway toward yet another stairwell.

Her footfalls echoed through the empty stairwell as she raced up two floors. The too-large boots she wore rubbed her heels, giving her blisters.

Reaching the door, she broke the locking mechanism and forced her way through as shouts echoed up the stairwell from below. Her pursuers were hot on her heels.

Karma sprinted down the hallway, following her nose, and shoved into the last room in the hallway. She shoved the woman in the lab coat who was leaving back in the room. She locked her arms around the woman's neck and head, squeezing until she passed out. Karma guided the woman to the floor and pulled her out of view of the small window.

The young girl strapped to the table yanked at the restraints, and wept. Annabeth.

Whatever they'd given her had knocked her for a loop.

Karma ripped the wrist restraints free and pried the metal clamps holding her feet until they could slide right through.

The instant her body was released from the restraints, Annabeth collapsed, her body giving out.

Karma caught Annabeth before she hit the ground and tossed her over her shoulder. She climbed onto the counter in the back corner and lifted the tile for the drop ceiling. It was a tight squeeze to heave them up onto the top of the wall. Karma's forearms burned.

Once through the hole, she balanced Annabeth against one of the steel supports for the floor above, turned back, and replaced the tile. She heaved Annabeth back onto her shoulder and snaked her way over, under, and through the steel trapezoid-shaped supports, while balancing on the tops of the walls below. She'd navigated this area many times, dodging plumbing and electrical pipes spanning from nearly every direction.

The shouts from below as they searched and failed to find her brought a smile to her face. She so enjoyed making their lives miserable.

It took longer than usual, with the added dead weight, but she eventually came upon the maintenance ladder she was looking for. Karma redistributed the weight and, careful not to drop Annabeth, climbed the metal rungs protruding from the concrete wall. She stopped on a familiar floor and retraced her usual path.

When she set her down at their destination, Annabeth's lips quivered, and whimpers escaped. Karma knelt to her level. "Shh. You have to be very quiet."

Annabeth flinched.

"I won't hurt you. I'm going to get you out of here."

Dropping through the ceiling tile she lifted, Karma stood on the top of a shelf in the storage room she used to get Ridge out of the building. She helped Annabeth down, then replaced the tile and set about making their escape.

While Annabeth didn't need to be carried now, she was unsteady on her bare and filthy feet, leaning heavily on Karma as they went.

Chapter 13

7619

Ridge

Ridge followed Peter through the secret door. At the end of the hallway, behind another secret door, was the kitchen of another trailer. They hadn't walked far, so it had to be the trailer next door to Karma's. The same rundown appearance, but still clean, and he could smell Karma and the girl, Lily, as well as Peter and another unfamiliar female within this trailer.

Peter lifted the rug on the kitchen floor and opened a door Ridge barely noticed, even after the rug had been lifted. Even his enhanced vision didn't help him see what was in the darkness below.

Peter motioned for Ridge to precede him into the tunnel, but kid or no, Ridge was too paranoid to allow someone unknown to walk behind him.

Peter just shrugged and bounced down the stairs.

Once Ridge reached the bottom, Peter walked back up and closed the trapdoor in the kitchen floor, then led the way back down the tunnel.

Impressed by the underground structure, he took in the smooth walls and floor, the supports, and the light filtering through a makeshift door to the side. With nowhere for the smells to go, the mystery woman from the second trailer's smell was the strongest underground. Pleasant humming reached his ears.

Just as they reached the door, Peter turned around and placed his hands on his hips, making himself look as large as possible. Ridge stifled a grin at Peter's attempt to make himself more intimidating.

"Rosie is a sweet lady. Be nice, or I'll make you leave."

Ridge wiped any trace of humor from his face and bent down to Peter's level. "I promise to be polite and respectful. I'm here to help keep you safe."

"I can keep us safe," he huffed. "I would never let anything happen to Rosie."

"Hey Peter," Ridge said conspiratorially, "I'm here only in case an Altered shows up. You know this place and the layout much better than I do. I'm going to rely on you to take care of Rosie while I handle anyone who shows up."

Peter nodded, determination and toughness settling solidly over his easily readable face. He turned and poked his head into the room, speaking louder than usual. "Rosie, I'm back! Karma asked me to bring her friend down while she went out to help Lily with the traps."

Ridge fought a smile at the stern look Peter gave him, his warning not to tell Rosie any other story.

Passing into the room, Ridge took in the smooth walls, the cots, and the threadbare sofa. He gave Rosie a warm smile and nodded to the weaving in her gnarled hands. "What are you making there?"

Rosie smiled and held up the large basket taking shape. "For Karma, when she goes shopping."

"We've made mats and rugs. They work okay as blankets, but they're best used in the baskets," Peter chimed in proudly.

Ridge stepped onto one of the plastic woven rugs on the floor, surprised at its plushness. He dropped to sit on the mat, listening to Peter and Rosie chatting about inane things, and observed his surroundings.

Rosie's skin was pale and grayish. She seemed frail, and, sitting as close as he was, he could hear her labored breathing. Curiously, he kept an eye on her, watching her labor more when she thought no one was watching.

He'd been lost in thought when she leaned forward and tapped him on the forearm.

"Cat?"

"Panther."

She hummed in interest. "You know what our Karma is?"

"Some kind of lizard, if her colder skin and the scales I've seen peek through her wounds are any clue."

"Komodo dragon."

Ridge sat stunned for a moment. It explained her strength and, as he reevaluated their surroundings, the digging. It should have taken crews of people months, if not years, to make a tunnel and room this size. For two young kids, an elderly lady, and Karma, it should've been impossible.

Hours later, Ridge still sat on the mat, listening to Rosie and Peter demonstrating how to weave. He'd been surprised at the stability of the earthen room during the aftershock. Rosie and Peter had barely flinched and kept on with their weaving as if nothing had happened.

A thud reached his ears, and he stood abruptly.

"Peter, you and Rosie stay here. I'm going to stretch my legs."

Peter eyed him warily. He placed the mat he was weaving beside him on the couch and stood too, placing himself between the doorway and Rosie.

Ridge nodded, stalking out into the tunnel and back toward the entrance. He reached the bottom of the stairs at the same moment the trapdoor lifted, and an overpowering stench wafted down to him. He pieced through the scents quickly and recognized a familiar smell beneath the foul odor permeating the air around her.

Lily stumbled back when she noticed him heading up the stairs.

Ridge put his hands up in surrender. "I'm not going to hurt you. Are you okay? Where's Karma?"

At the mention of Karma's name, Lily sobbed and dropped to her knees on the kitchen floor.

He closed the distance, leaping up the last few stairs, and shut the trapdoor. Ridge couldn't see through the half-dried muck covering Lily's body to see if there were injuries.

"Are you hurt?" he asked calmly.

Lily shook her head.

He could work with that. Ridge tugged on her hand to get her to her feet and walked her to the bathroom down the hall, where he'd noticed barrels of water already waiting to be used. "Get yourself clean, then you can tell me what happened."

Lily gave him a skeptical look.

"Karma left me here to protect Peter and Rosie until she returned. I'll help in whatever way I can."

When Lily came out of the bathroom a little bit later, the smell threatening to deaden his nose was much more subtle. He'd opened the windows in the trailer to help air it out and made some food, placing it on the battered table to the side of the kitchen.

She moved around the trailer, giving him as wide a berth as possible, then sat at the table and dug in as if she hadn't eaten all day.

He waited until her eating slowed, not wanting to spook her. He kept his voice calm, despite the urgency pushing at him in his gut. "Lily, did Karma find you, or did you get back on your own?"

Tears filled her eyes, but she swallowed hard, not letting them fall. "She found me. She got me out. But she couldn't leave." The last word broke on a sob, and the tears fell in earnest.

Ridge didn't know what to do with tears and awkwardly patted her hand, trying to offer some comfort to the young lady, little more than a child who had to grow up too fast. He cleared his throat. "Out of where? Where were you?"

He dreaded the answer he knew was coming.

"Phoenix Corps."

"Shit!" He burst to his feet, anxiety and fear ramping his heart rate up. Ridge flexed his fingers as his claws itched to be unsheathed. He shook his head clear, pushed down the panic, and took his seat. His voice calm again, he said, "What did they do to you? Are you certain you are okay?"

"I don't think I was in there for more than a few hours. They injected me with something, and they took a lot of blood, but they didn't have time to do much before Karma came."

Ridge waited for her to continue.

"I left the trailer park to look for meat in our traps. Karma told me not to, but the trailer park traps were all empty. Annabeth wanted to come with me, so I figured it would be safe with both of us."

The guilt filling her eyes hit Ridge in the heart, and he covered her hands with his. "We all make dumb mistakes. I'm not sure if you know, but I took some meat from a trap that wasn't mine. Whew! I was in big trouble. Practically took it from a kid, too." He shook his head shamefully. "Luckily, they showed me mercy. Even helped to take care of me when I was hurt."

A shy smile slid over Lily's face. "It was pretty stupid to steal from Karma." She absently spun her spoon around on the table. "Karma comes for everyone eventually."

Ridge swallowed hard at the imagery floating through his brain at that statement.

Lily continued, "I rounded the corner, almost to the store to recheck those traps, when two of the goon squad pounced on us. A big, burly guy, rough, tough and stupid, and the girl was just as mean, but smarter. They were both altered. Karma taught me how to defend myself, but I'm not effective against Altereds.

"I apparently put up enough of a fight that they knocked me out, because the next thing I knew, I was in the back of a big box truck, tied up next to Annabeth, with the girl watching me, daring me to try something." Lily shivered against the memory.

Ridge consciously loosened the tension in his hands. If he ever got his hands on the goon squad... "What happened then?" he asked through gritted teeth.

"When they got us to Phoenix Corps, they dragged me down to a room and tied me to a table in the dark. I didn't see where they took Annabeth. They apparently didn't like my screaming and tied a gag around my mouth." Lily pointed at the bruising at the corners of her mouth and cheeks.

Looking closer, he could see wounds beneath the bruising. It set his teeth on edge. She was just a kid. She couldn't fight back. *Not like he could.* His mind stuttered on that thought. Yes, he was only one guy. Maybe the time had come to let Phoenix Corps know he wasn't dead, and he was going to come for them. Karma had been fighting since she left.

She didn't need to fight alone.

"I don't know how long I was on that table. Whatever they injected me with made me a bit woozy, and like I said, they took a lot of blood. It wasn't long after the aftershock when Karma snuck into the lab they held me in."

Ridge listened to the tale, completely unsurprised by every move Karma made, including getting her ward free by staying behind. When Lily finished, he stood. "Are you up to protecting Peter and Rosie?" he asked.

Her eyes met his, determination and stubbornness shining through. "Yes."

If the physical differences weren't so vast, Lily could've been Karma's daughter. He'd seen that exact look on her face.

"You go down, say hi to them, and do what you usually do when Karma leaves you in charge. I'll go see what I can do to bring her home."

In a completely unexpected move, Lily threw her arms around Ridge, hugging him tight. "Thank you!"

The moment Lily was ensconced in the earthen room with the others, Ridge was headed out of the park.

It had been nearly twelve hours since Karma left him at the trailer to go find Lily. He felt much better, much stronger, but still not one hundred percent. Between the nasty infection and the blood loss, he'd been knocked out of commission far more than he had since the torment Phoenix Corps had put him through.

It wasn't a sound that drew his attention when he passed an alleyway not far from the service road. It was a smell.

Ridge turned down the alley and stalked through the knee-deep trash.

The scent got stronger, overpowering the smells of the trash covering the alley floor. He turned to look back the way he came and was rewarded with a hard shoulder to his gut, driving him back against a crumbling brick wall behind him.

Despite her small frame, she managed to wedge her forearm against his neck, pinning him in place.

He couldn't help the smirk on his face when he said, "Hey Karma. I was just looking for you." His voice strained from the pressure she applied.

"Why are you here? You left them?" Her tone was incredulous, and violence swirled in her eyes.

"She's back, cleaned up, and I left her in charge to rescue you. She said you stayed behind." The pressure on his neck eased as he spoke, and Karma backed off.

"She made it home?" The relief in her voice was palpable, but a warning lurked in her eyes that he couldn't decipher.

Ridge nodded. "I left her in charge and with food." He took a deep breath and regretted it immediately. "Use the same sewer?" he asked, covering his nose with his shirt.

"To get in, yes. To get out, I used the path I carried your ass through."

"Ahh, that's why the stench is more muted than hers." Movement at the corner of his eye caught his attention.

A young blonde who needed at least twenty more pounds on her to be healthy stared at him with wide, terrified eyes.

He turned his questioning gaze to Karma.

"This is Annabeth. Head back the way you came and tell them that we will have a visitor."

He bristled at the order. But, when he looked, really looked, at Karma, the hunch in her shoulders, the dark smudges under her eyes, a strange, almost gray-green pallor to her skin, he softened. She'd spent the last few days barely getting any sleep and taking care of him, then rescuing Lily, and now Annabeth. "Why don't you go ahead? I'll help Anna-beth."

The girl gasped in fear and clung to Karma's arm like a life raft.

"Or you continue with the rescue, and I'll go let them know you're on your way."

Karma gave him a tired smile. "Thanks."

Ridge turned and headed back the way he came.

Chapter 14

5713

Karma

Lily made it home.

Taking a roundabout way to mask their easy-to-fol-
low scent, it was over an hour before Karma entered
the trailer park. The sun was high in the sky, and the
temperature and humidity rose to uncomfortable
levels. The gross muck from the tunnels dried and
cracked over her skin and stolen clothes. Her nose
was rendered useless by her own stench.

By the time her trailer came into view, Ridge was
leaning in the doorway, like he belonged there. His
large frame filled the door, and his relaxed pose
belied his attention to detail. The squeeze in her
heart at the sight worried her. *Was she really happy*

he was here? She couldn't afford to lose sight of her goal. Karma was going to end Phoenix Corps if it was the last thing she ever did.

She did her damnedest to piss them off at every turn. Some may believe she'd been dead or long gone, like Biff said. But, even when they weren't sure it had been her, they suspected. Pip always suspected. She'd just confirmed twice to him that she was there in the span of a few days.

Ridge stepped to the side, clearing space for Karma and Annabeth to enter.

"There's water in the bathroom, Annabeth. Go clean up first. We'll get you some food."

Karma raised her eyebrow at Ridge taking charge like he lived there.

He just shrugged and stepped out of the way. "There's fresh water in the other bathroom for you. I had it filled while I brought water here for Annabeth. I assume you want her to stay in this trailer for a bit."

Karma barely had the energy left to nod. Now that she was safe, in her home, the sheer stubbornness keeping her going drained out.

Karma yelped in surprise as she was lifted off her feet.

"You're limping," he growled.

"Happens when you've walked, run, and climbed in shoes way too big for your feet," Karma said flatly. "Now put me down." The order came out harsher than she intended, but the flutter in her belly at his proximity made her clench every muscle to keep from melting against him.

She didn't need anyone. Karma was strong and capable.

Ridge tightened his hold on her, ignoring her order. Then he must have thought better of it, because he set her gently on her feet. "Go get cleaned up. I'll keep an eye on your newest guest." He tentatively reached out, laying his warm hand on her shoulder. "Lily has been worried. If she isn't already in the other trailer, you should pop down and see her."

Her heart melted at the compassion and warmth in his voice. She nodded, unable to speak past the lump in her throat.

Karma took one step toward the door and stopped. She bent over, tearing one offensive boot off, then the other, tossing them in the bin of garbage they would soon burn. She dusted her grubby hands on her equally grimy pants and walked out of the trailer.

Letting herself into Mrs. Thorn's old trailer, she stopped first in the bathroom to clean up, changing into worn jeans and a faded blue T-shirt. An inspection of her feet had her cringing. The osteoderms of her Komodo Dragon skin poked through the places where the human skin had worn away.

She grumbled as she pulled on thick socks and her last pair of sneakers. She'd need to go shopping again.

When she emerged from the bathroom, Lily fell into her arms, sobbing.

"I'm sorry. I'm so sorry." Lily repeated over and over.

"Hey," Karma said, lifting Lily's face from her shoulder so she could look into her eyes. "I'm safe. You're safe. It's okay."

Lily sniffed, wiping her wet cheeks with her hands.

"Annabeth?"

Karma nodded. She made sure her tone was gentle yet firm when she spoke again. "Next time I tell you to stay in the trailer park, *stay in the trailer park*, *even* when there isn't any meat in the traps here. Okay?"

Lily buried her head in her shoulder, and Karma held her until the sobs subsided.

"Ridge took good care of them while we were away. Peter and Rosie both said so."

"I'm glad," Karma said cautiously.

"Other than the first encounter, he's been nothing but nice."

"Uh huh."

"Will he come and stay here? At the park? " Lily's questions and statements came in rapid succession. "He could help when you and I are out. Or when you are out. Or *he* can go shopping."

Karma smiled. "He won you over, did he?"

Lily blushed clear to her hairline. "Rosie and Peter agree. You can't do it all, Karma. He could help."

"He probably doesn't *want* to help, Lil. He's been on his own a long time. Besides, we have enough on our plates without adding more."

"He could help with the plate!"

Karma changed the subject, unwilling to voice how much she liked the idea of him staying, taking some of her burden. She could, and would, do it on her own, like she had for the last ten years. "I need you, Peter, and Rosie to continue using this entrance. Until I say otherwise, you stay here and stay hidden. Got it?"

Lily nodded solemnly. "Is Annabeth okay?"

"I got her out. We'll keep an eye on her. But only you, Peter, Rosie, and Ridge now know about the tunnel and this trailer. I want to keep it that way. So, don't use the hallway to enter my trailer." Karma gave her one last hug and sent her back into the tunnel. She raced back out and around the trailer, returning to her own kitchen.

Ridge had a can of soup, hot and waiting for her.

She took it gratefully and sat on her threadbare couch, waiting for Annabeth to emerge from the bathroom.

"Where did you find her?" he asked, tilting his head to indicate the young woman in the bathroom.

"In a lab, on my way out of there. She was with Lily when they were taken. She lives on the edge of the trailer park."

"You aren't taking her back to her own place?"

"She's alone there. I don't know what they did to the girls while they had them in their custody. We need to watch them closely for a couple of days."

"How many times have you broken into Phoenix Corps?"

"Countless."

"How many people have you brought out with you?"

"As many as a dozen a year. Most times, fewer."

"And they still haven't caught you?"

"It's not like I've gone far. I'm staying in the same trailer as I did before the quake. They've apparently thought me too bright to come back here and ignored it, or they haven't been smart enough to check the forms I had to sign when I went to them for help nine years ago." Karma shrugged and set her now-empty can on the small wooden table in front of the sofa. "I have several different ways in and out. They don't usually know I've been in there when I am stealing food, clothing, and supplies. When I leave with one of their victims, I lie low for a bit. After a few weeks, they get lax again, and I wander in with no one the wiser."

Ridge looked impressed. A moment later, his head tipped, listening, then nodded down the hallway where Annabeth was emerging from the bathroom.

Karma stood, meeting her partway down the hall and taking the soiled linens from her arms. "I'll burn these. There's some food for you on the counter. Sit and enjoy it. I'll be back in just a moment." She dropped the now-useless rags on top of her stolen boots and hauled the bin outside, letting the door slam behind her.

After dropping the contents of the bin into the large steel barrel, Karma set the contents ablaze.

Once the initial flare of the fire settled, she reentered the trailer and stood by the kitchen window to keep an eye on the flames.

"Did they just take blood? Or did they inject you with anything?" Karma asked.

"They injected me with something right away. It made me a bit loopy. I don't remember much after that, until you came in." Her jaw cracked with a wide yawn.

"You can rest in there," Karma said, pointing to the room where Ridge had been recovering. "I'll be within shouting distance if you need anything at all."

"I can't go home?"

"You shouldn't be alone right now, Annabeth. Whatever you were injected with, your body could react to it, and if you are alone and need help... You should stay here until we are sure you won't have a reaction."

"Where's Lily? Shouldn't she be here for you to keep an eye on, too?"

"Lily is being watched over, too."

"I want to go home. I don't want to stay here."

"While I understand that, what will you do if you spike a fever? If you are too weak to come get me? Or would you rather I stay with you in your trailer?"

"Or, how about you show some appreciation for the risk Karma had to take to get you out of there." Ridge's tone held barely suppressed rage, a fire burning in his mesmerizing green eyes, as he stared Annabeth down.

Annabeth stood as if to storm out, wobbled on her feet, then lowered her chin, placing her empty can next to Karma's. "Thank you. For everything."

Karma nodded.

The old bed creaked when Annabeth climbed in, and Karma's eyes drooped heavily.

"Go rest," Ridge prodded.

"Go home."

Ridge stepped up to her, too close. He placed his hand on her cheek.

Her body betrayed her, leaning into his touch, into the comfort he offered.

"You haven't slept in days. You were up, taking care of me, then breaking and entering. You rescued two people from the clutches of Phoenix Corps, and you're injured on top of that."

"I'm fine."

"'You're practically dead on your feet. Rest."

"Annabeth..."

"Will sleep for a few hours. I'll watch over her. You head down with the others and get some rest. I heard you and Lily talking. But I know Peter and Rosie would like to see you for themselves." His thumb continued to caress her cheek.

Her eyelids grew heavier with each pass. She shook her head, both to deny her need for sleep and to dislodge his hand and the disconcerting feelings it caused.

"You trusted me with Peter and Rosie. With Lily. Trust me now. You don't have to do it all."

Karma still couldn't say why she trusted him. She barely knew him. But he was right. She trusted he would protect them.

"Annabeth doesn't know you," she argued.

"You won't be a help to anyone if you are exhausted. And you won't fight as well either. You want Pip getting the upper hand next time, pet?"

Her hand shot out lightning fast, aiming to grab him by the throat. But, in her exhaustion, he was faster, clutching her hand within his own.

"See?"

"Fine." Karma yanked her hand away and spun for the door. Before she reached for the handle, she shot him a look over her shoulder. "Exhausted or not, if you call me 'pet' again, I'll make sure it's the last time."

Chapter 15

5713

Karma

Thundering down the earth and stone stairs in the tunnel jolted her awake. Karma jumped to her feet and barreled into the tunnel to meet the threat before it entered the room with Lily, Peter, and Rosie.

Ridge stood in front of her, his chest heaving.

"What's wrong?"

"Annabeth. There's something wrong with her." Ridge spun on his heel and darted back up the stairs, not waiting for her to follow.

On his heels, Karma trailed behind, surprised, but grateful he'd walked along the exterior of the trailers to get her, rather than expose the hidden hallway door.

"Is she feverish? Seizing?"

"Definitely a high fever. She's thrashing, but I'm not sure I'd say it was a seizure, more like a fever dream."

"Is there still water in the bathroom?"

He nodded.

She ripped the door to her trailer open and headed straight for the room Annabeth occupied. "Bring me a pan of water and a clean rag. A glass of drinking water, too, please." Karma didn't wait for him to respond. She knelt next to the cot, holding Annabeth, and placed a hand on her burning skin.

Annabeth moaned in agony and pulled away from her touch. She thrashed.

"Shhh," Karma soothed, "You're safe, Annabeth. No one will harm you here. You are safe."

More brutal thrashing was the only response.

Karma surged to her feet and grabbed her last length of rope. Last shoes, last rope. She shook her head and headed back into the room, securing Annabeth much like she had Ridge.

He returned just as Annabeth caught Karma off guard with a hard kick to her solar plexus, doubling her over. Ridge was at her side in a flash, pinning Annabeth to the cot so Karma could secure the rope.

"She's stronger than she should be for her size," he observed.

"Could be adrenaline..." Karma trailed off. She moved up to Annabeth's arms after securing her feet.

"All this after a few hours in their custody?"

"We don't know what they injected her or Lily with. She could be *very* sick for a while. Fevers, seizures, rashes. I've seen organ failure happen quickly, too. She'll either fight through it and come out on top or she won't."

"If she comes through?"

"They didn't have her long, so hopefully there won't be any lasting effects. But they've improved their techniques over the last decade. She should still be in her safe window. "

"And, if not?"

"I'll have to kill her." Her voice was quiet; anyone with normal hearing would never have heard, but Ridge stiffened. Karma dropped her eyes. Shame flushed over her.

He closed the distance between them. "She'd be a danger to herself, to Lily, Peter, and Rosie, and to the rest of the people living in this trailer park that I've not seen but have certainly smelled."

Karma nodded.

Ridge's large, warm, and calloused hand landed on her shoulder and squeezed as he bent down to her level. "You have taken on the responsibility of this entire community, their safety, their hunger, their well-being. Not many people would do what you've done. Phoenix Corps is what most people do."

The overwhelming desire to lean into his strength stole her breath. Her eyes closed as his hand moved to glide over her neck and up to her cheek, cradling her face. She couldn't help the tremor that stole over her body.

His breath whispered over her lips as he closed the distance between their mouths.

Peter's shout had her ripping away from his hold and dashing from her trailer.

Tears streamed down Peter's cheeks. "Lily's sick." Terror shook his voice.

Peter's words stole her breath. She'd gotten to Lily quickly, but not quickly enough.

Her feet were moving, carrying her back to the tunnel, Annabeth completely forgotten.

Lighting a lantern as soon as her feet touched down in the tunnel, Karma rushed into the room and took in the scene before her. Lily thrashed on the cot. No sweat glistened on her skin, which was hot and dry to the touch.

"Peter, bring me a bucket with some water, a rag, and a glass." Her gaze caught on Ridge, who'd followed her. "Take Rosie upstairs and get her settled in this trailer. Then come back. I'll show you the best places to put the water to cool them down. I'll do my best to go back and forth, but the sooner we cool them both down, the better."

Karma grabbed the supplies from Peter as soon as he reentered the room. The poor kid was terrified, white as a sheet, with eyes the size of saucers. Peter had grown again, she noticed, now right at her height, barely a teen, but he was still so much a child.

She tipped his chin with her thumb, so their eyes met. "I need you to keep Rosie calm and safe, okay, buddy?" At his nod, she continued, "I'm going to get her better. And while I do, I need you to help out

Rosie. Keep her in Mrs. Thorn's trailer for now. I'll be back and forth to check on you guys, okay?"

He nodded his head again, his overly long, dirty-blond hair bobbing with the movement.

Karma ruffled that hair. "Thanks for your help, Peter."

"Good job, bud," Ridge said, patting him on the shoulder as he walked past.

Karma caught a glimpse of the pride beaming from Peter's face at Ridge's praise, and her breath hitched.

Their eyes collided for a split second before she turned her attention to Lily, still in the throes of a feverish nightmare, and her temperature rising.

The sun barely peeked over the horizon, visibility obscured by the constant presence of dust and debris floating high in the atmosphere. Karma hardly noticed as she trudged on tired legs back to her trailer for what had to be the hundredth time since she'd been alerted by Ridge of Annabeth's fever.

She knocked quietly and entered her trailer. Ridge's scent had permeated every inch of her trailer until it was all she could smell. She fought back the tears of frustration and stifled her desire to curl up next to him and put all her responsibilities behind her for a while. His glowing green eyes pierced her from the couch, watching her with a predator's eyes, discerning her every weakness. Her breath hitched with the impact of his gaze.

All in one breath, she wanted to cower and slide as close as she could get. Gathering her strength like a shield around her, she straightened and walked to the doorway of the room Annabeth occupied. She cleared her throat to speak around the lump lodged there, full of the things she wouldn't allow herself to say to him. "How is she?" Her voice betrayed her exhaustion.

"She's stopped thrashing. I think the fever is lower. She doesn't feel as hot to the touch." Ridge's breath fanned over her ear, standing too close for her comfort, but not close enough either. "The mud you packed around her seemed to help. But that mattress is too filthy to use after this."

She fought her body's reaction to his proximity, the urge to lean into him, into his strength, nearly overwhelming. She tensed as his large, calloused hand came to rest on the small of her back, fighting her desire to melt at the comfort he offered. "It was too filthy after you. Between the mud and the blood, there's nothing to save it. I covered what I could, but it's what we have on hand right now." Her gaze scanned over Annabeth, lying limp and pale on the cot. "Her wrists are raw," she observed tightly.

"Fighting against the restraints. She's stronger than she looks."

Karma nodded sadly. "Her fever dreams were much more violent than Lily's."

She bent down and untied the knots of rope at Annabeth's right and left arms, then gently cleaned the areas that had been rubbed raw. No sign of altered skin showed through the damage. Karma left the ropes on the bed, within reach.

"Leave the ropes off unless she fights or thrashes. The less pain we can inflict, the better."

"How is Lily?" he asked, his voice soft.

She met his eyes for a moment, jolted by the intensity she saw there, and she quickly lowered them again. "Her fever is down. They only had her for a few hours. They couldn't have done more than a couple of shots of who knows what. She said they took blood, probably to run tests to see which animal she'd be most compatible with. Hopefully, this is just a reaction to the injections they got."

Karma retraced her steps, careful not to touch Ridge as she went through the doorway into the kitchen. She busied herself, heating another can of soup.

Ridge ran his fingers over the healing wounds on her arm from Pip, and she fought unsuccessfully to hide the tremble his touch elicited. His fingers trailed slowly up her arm, over her throat, and she swallowed hard.

The can she was holding dented, cracking loudly through the silent room.

She turned her head, meeting his vivid green eyes, the intensity there threatening to bring her to her knees. Her brain screamed predator, danger. Her body screamed arousal, urging submission. Her heart melted just a little more, whispering trust, companionship. She closed her eyes against the warring feelings and took stock of her instincts. Her gut she trusted.

Chapter 16

7619

Ridge

Her eyes fluttered closed.

Ridge let his hand continue its journey, burying it-self in her silky hair, tightening on the nape of her neck, tilting her face to his. He claimed her lips, tentatively first, waiting for her to strike out at him.

Her small sigh was an electric cattle prod to his body. He pulled her tight to his body, cocooning her in his embrace.

By appearance, she was small, weak. The strength in her arms as they banded around him in answer belied that delicate appearance.

He deepened the kiss, changing the angle of his head, turning her body, pinning her against the kitchen counter with his. Her scent drove him wild. Her strength, her sense of responsibility, and determination were admirable. The care she paid to others, the sacrifices she made—he'd never met another person like her.

He sucked in her bottom lip, biting it lightly, drawing out another sigh. His fingers toyed with the skin he exposed, lifting the hem of her shirt, caressing the smooth skin of her stomach, reveling in the tremors radiating out from his touch. He itched to claim her completely, to make her his. Right here, on this counter, but a whimper from the other room registered, and he reluctantly pulled away.

Ridge dropped his forehead to hers, both of them breathing raggedly. He smoothed her shirt back down into place. He bent, wanting one last touch of her lips in a sweet kiss, but was unable to stop himself from the tender, lingering kiss it evolved into.

His voice growly and guttural, he said, "I'll check on the patient and let you finish with the soup." Ridge sauntered into the other room, adjusting to make himself more comfortable in the jeans he wore.

5713

Karma

Feeling flushed, Karma blew out her breath and tried to calm her quaking hands. They trembled as she set about heating food for Annabeth. Ridge's rough yet soothing voice reached her ears as he spoke softly to Annabeth, reassuring her that she was safe.

She'd been helpless in her response to him. Her body had betrayed her. She had betrayed Dorian's memory. Her body still buzzed from the connection with Ridge, demanding she finish what he started. She clenched her fists, digging her blunt nails into the skin of her palms until they caused pain.

Karma felt her world spinning out of control. Pip, Phoenix Corps, their damn goon squad, Lily and Annabeth sick, Peter and Rosie to care for. She could lean on him. He could help take some things off her plate, like Lily said.

She shook her head. Karma wouldn't rely on him, wouldn't rely on anyone again. She was responsible for her own life, her own safety. Relying on someone else only made her weak, vulnerable.

Karma set two cans of warmed soup on the counter and quietly slipped out with the others. She delivered two more cans to Peter and Rosie, then entered the tunnel with the final can for Lily.

Lily slept peacefully, a light glistening of sweat coating her, reflecting the light from the lantern, proof that the fever was breaking, and hopefully on its way to being completely gone.

Lying a hand on Lily's head, she was rewarded with cooler skin and a soft sigh.

Lily's eyes opened and gazed around the room, her brow wrinkling.

"Stay still," Karma instructed. "You've had a high fever. I've made you some soup to eat, and I want you to drink a full glass of water, then you can rest again for a while."

Lily struggled to sit up. "I feel so weak."

"They injected you with something while they had you. Your body is fighting it off."

"Am I going to turn...?" Lily started.

"Oh no, sweetheart. You'll be fine, I promise. You weren't there long, and you won't go back. I won't let them have you." Her voice started melodic and soft. By the time she finished, her voice was stern, unyielding, and fierce.

Lily took the spoon, her hand shaking, and Karma took it back.

"Sit back against the wall. I'll help you get started. That fever took a lot for your body to fend off. It will take a bit before you are back in fighting shape."

A sad smile stole over Lily's face. "I'm sorry."

Karma fed her a spoonful of soup. "You've learned your lesson and then some. Nothing to be sorry about. We'll get through this as we have gotten through everything else."

A while later, Peter stood at the entrance of the room. "Ridge left for a while. Said he'd be back soon. Annabeth is sleeping again." His eyes dropped to where Lily lay, once again sleeping.

Karma easily read the worry there. "She's gonna be fine, Peter."

His eyes darted between Karma and Lily.

She could see the wheels turning in his brain, trying to determine if she was sugarcoating it for him. "You can help me get Rosie back here in a bit, so you two can keep an eye on Lily for me, while I sit with Annabeth."

Hope blossomed in his eyes, and a smile lit his face. He nodded eagerly, bouncing on his toes.

With Rosie and Peter settled back in with a sleeping Lily, Karma headed back to her trailer. Ridge's scent caused a swarm of butterflies to scatter in her belly. She closed her eyes, resting her hand on the door to gather her wits, then opened the door, walking in.

Annabeth rested peacefully on the cot. Her fever was still high, but the restlessness was currently absent. Ridge had cleaned the kitchen before leaving, so Karma walked to the uncomfortable couch and lay down, throwing her forearm over her eyes. Maybe she could rest for just a minute.

While sleep claimed her in short order, restful it was not.

Ridge was still here in her dreams, their encounter in the kitchen not interrupted. His hands on her, his mouth. The softness of his hair tangled in her fingers, the sharpness of his teeth as he nipped at her lips and throat. Her body arched up in her sleep, her audible moan waking her.

Emptiness filled her with the realization that she was in her trailer with only a sick Annabeth to keep her company. Karma turned her face into the couch, the rough fabric scratching over her skin. It smelled like him. He must have spent most of his time sitting in this exact spot, watching over Annabeth, while she tended to Lily.

She heard Annabeth moving around and stood to check on her.

Annabeth panted with the effort it took to sit up.

Karma rushed to her side to help.

Annabeth's skin, while cooler to the touch than it had been, was still uncomfortably warm to Karma's naturally lower body temperature.

"You still have a fever and are weak. You should stay in bed."

She gulped air with the effort to sit up. "Bathroom."

Karma helped Annabeth to her feet, taking most of her weight, and situated her in the bathroom. "You alright on your own in here?"

Annabeth nodded, pallor evident on her face. "I might be a while, but I'll be fine."

"Shout if you need me. I'll be right out here." Karma backed out and pulled the door shut behind her.

Karma spent some time weaving while she waited. When Annabeth called out to her, she helped her back into bed and got her to drink another glass of water before laying her down to rest again. She was so weak that Karma needed to take nearly all her weight to help her get back to bed.

Once Annabeth was tucked back in, Karma checked on Lily and the others, who were doing fine, and retreated to her trailer once again.

Chapter 17

Karma

The smell of fresh, cooking meat pulled her from sleep.

Ridge stood in the kitchen, and she shot to her feet.

"What are you doing back? How did you get in here? How did I miss it? What are you doing? Where did you get meat?" Her questions fired off one after another, giving him no time to actually answer any of them.

He stepped around the counter and laid his hands on her shoulders, ignoring her intake of breath at the contact. "I stole from your traps again. The least I can do to help is bring you some food. You have been feeding me after all. I am cooking. I was quiet, and you were passed out from lack of sleep, I'd imagine. I picked your lock, which is *very* flimsy, by the way. And I told Peter I'd be back soon." He'd answered every one of her questions in reverse order.

She paid close attention to every word coming out of his mouth, so she didn't pay attention to the way his shirt pulled tight across his shoulders, his scent—his own distinct and spicy smell--the timbre of his voice.

Using his considerable height and strength, Ridge pressed her down onto the sofa. "I've got dinner covered. You keep resting." A playful wink followed, then he turned, striding the few steps into the kitchen, giving her a mouthwatering view of his butt in his well-worn, well-fitting jeans as he walked away.

Now that she was awake, he hummed a little as he worked.

She picked up her weaving but spent most of her time stealing glances at him from beneath her lashes.

When dinner finished cooking, Ridge brought her an old, chipped plate she hadn't used in years, piled high with meat and greens. She started to protest the amount, but he leveled her with a look. "You didn't eat anything yet today. You can't take care of the people you need to if you don't take care of yourself."

She hadn't realized he'd noticed.

"Sit and eat. I'll check on Annabeth."

As she listened to the rumble of his voice from the other room, Karma took her first bite. Spices burst in her mouth at the first taste, and she couldn't stifle the groan of satisfaction.

"I like that sound." His voice, rougher than usual, caused her to look up, seeing him leaning against the door frame, a cocky expression on his chiseled face.

She swallowed hard, trying to hide her reaction to the timbre of his voice, which felt like a physical caress. "Where did you get spices?"

"The badger I told you about had a few spice plants that do well in very little light. He was kind enough to give me some of his stock and an overview of how to care for them myself. I have a decent stockpile. I'll be sure to bring you some."

His languid smile caused her heart rate to speed up. Karma could only nod. Forming words required brain power that his every move seemed to disrupt.

He delivered another plate to Annabeth and then took plates to the others. The respite from his presence allowed her heart to settle back into its normal rhythm.

When he reentered the trailer, he sat next to her on the couch. Ridge wrapped his arm around her shoulder and pulled her closer, tucking her into his side.

"You're not eating?" she managed to say as her nerves went haywire at the sensations his closeness brought. The warmth, solid muscle, strength, and security made her want to lean in further, let him take some of the burden.

"I'm good for now."

His fingers toyed with the hair hanging past her shoulders, causing delicious shivers.

She closed her eyes and pulled in a ragged breath. Anxiety spiked, and the walls seemed to close in around her. Karma jumped to her feet, took her plate to the kitchen, and proceeded to clean.

"I'll take care of that."

"No. The cook shouldn't have to clean," she rushed to say, keeping her eyes glued to the dishes on the counter.

Ridge penned her into the kitchen, blocking her from any escape, but giving her a few inches of breathing room. "I get your nervousness. I'm patient. I'm not going anywhere." His hand drifted down her cheek, cupping her chin, and tilted her face so she had no choice but to look at him. "I'm not going anywhere, Karma."

She swallowed hard at the fierce determination and heat in his eyes—eyes that threatened to drown her in their depths.

He gave her a sly grin and backed away, as if it weren't an electrically charged space filled with tension, and returned a moment later with Annabeth's plate. Ridge exited the room again just as quickly, leaving the trailer presumably to get the plates from the others.

Her suspicions proved correct when he deposited the other plates on the counter, dropped a kiss to her forehead, and left as quickly as he came, humming happily the whole way.

Karma stood there, motionless, her mind whirring. The trailer felt empty without him. *How in just a few days had she become so used to his presence that it felt lonelier when he was gone?*

She shook the thought from her head. There were too many people counting on her. She couldn't afford a distraction, and Ridge was a *massive* distraction.

When the dishes were back in their proper places, Karma checked on Annabeth and found her sleeping. She did a quick check to find Lily sitting up, playing a game with Peter. They talked incessantly about Ridge, his meal, and when they hoped he'd return.

Karma walked the perimeter of the trailer park, not only looking for out-of-place scents but checking on Jacob, Judy, and the others.

Ridge had indeed taken at least some of the meat he cooked from the traps around the trailer park. Several were empty but had fresh smells on them—and Ridge's scent permeated the air. Though she had to admit, some of that irresistible smell could be from her and her clothing, since they'd been so close earlier. She shook her head again, trying to dislodge him from protruding into her thoughts, and frustration built.

Dusk crept up, and she headed back to the trailer. Annabeth still dozed but was restless again. From the heat radiating from her, the fever was back. This could go on for days, sapping Annabeth's energy. It would be a rollercoaster for the foreseeable future.

Karma left her trailer to check on Lily, and what she found brought tears to her eyes. Lily's face was pale, her closed eyes so dark they looked bruised.

Peter had already draped cool, wet rags over her, as he'd seen Karma do. Fear and concern swirled in his eyes. He should be out playing with friends, not hiding here.

Anger at the whole situation boiled her blood, but she pushed it down. "We've seen this before. She will probably have fevers for a few days off and on. Lily is as tough as they come." Karma set up everything they would need, so it was close at hand. "If she gets worse, Peter, come get me. I need to get back up to Annabeth. She's in rougher shape. I'll be back as often as I can to check on Lily."

Annabeth was back to thrashing violently.

Karma retied the rope and placed wet compresses on her blazing skin, re-dampening the mud she'd packed against Annabeth as well. It seemed like days before Annabeth's temperature lowered to the point that the thrashing and fever dreams lessened, but it was still dark outside when Karma was able to release the ties and leave the room. Without rest, she checked on Lily, who was still sleeping peacefully, though the fever still consumed her. She quietly changed the damp rags, so as not to wake Rosie or Peter, and managed to get Lily to drink a bit. As Lily returned to sleep, Karma returned to the trailer to keep vigil over Annabeth.

She prepared food, noticing the sky beginning to lighten. Karma checked on Lily again when she delivered the food.

Still pale, Lily's skin was cooler, and she was able to sit up in bed and feed herself.

Karma returned to the trailer soon after. Annabeth was still unconscious, but her temperature had dropped slightly. Eating would take more energy than Karma had. She plopped face down onto the couch and sighed. Asleep almost instantly, she still had enough brain power to notice Ridge's scent still lingering.

Chapter 18

7619

Ridge

Ridge tossed and turned on his rough cot. He itched to return to the trailer park. But Karma was obviously uncomfortable with what was developing between them. He wanted to give her the space he thought she needed. He'd been happy to cook for her, take care of her.

With a rough growl, he pushed himself up and threw his boots back on. He pulled on the leather jacket he'd taken from Phoenix Corps when he escaped. Well-worn in spots, the black jacket fit well, kept him warm, and worked as a barrier for defense.

Ridge's first stop was the garden where he kept his herbs. They grew best in a small, raised bed he'd managed to construct in the ruins of a building a few blocks from his home. On occasion, he'd notice a plant or two missing, but whoever was "shopping" from him was courteous and left the majority alone.

Several people meandered the streets, warily watching everyone they came across, slinking between buildings and piles of rubble at every chance. Ridge smelled a few others, but people kept their distance in general. Trust was a limited commodity.

By now, people scattered and hid like insects the moment they heard noises, just in case it was a member of the goon squad.

The large, worn, wooden box he'd pieced together weighed a ton by the time he'd gathered all the things he would need and headed to the trailer park.

Heavier than usual haze hung in the air, dulling further the already weakened light of the sun. He came into the area from another entrance, startling a few of what he assumed were regular residents. They scurried out of sight, but the hairs on the back of his neck stood on end, as he walked deeper into the compound.

Approaching Karma's trailer, where her scent was strongest, Ridge knocked very lightly. He knew her hearing wasn't as good as his. The sound of his knocking wouldn't wake her if she was sleeping, but she probably could hear it if she was awake.

When no response came, he picked the lock, noting that he'd need to scavenge a better one to replace it with. Karma slept soundly on the couch, and a glance in the bedroom revealed Annabeth heavily sleeping as well.

He backed out, re-securing the door, and carried the box to the other trailer. Ridge heard Peter moving around inside and knocked, announcing his presence.

With a smile, Peter opened the door for him.

"How did your night go?" Ridge asked.

Peter's easy smile fell, and he shook his head. "Lily got sick again. And so did Annabeth. Karma was so busy all night. There were some dishes by Lily's bed, so she must have come in a couple of times while Rosie and I were sleeping."

"How is Lily now?"

"She's still resting, but her fever is down. Rosie is sitting with her now." Peter eyed the box sitting on the ground behind Ridge. "What's all that?"

"Care to give me a hand on a project?"

Excitement and pride lit Peter's eyes. His chest puffed out a bit, and he nodded eagerly. "Yes, sir! What can I do?"

"Go tell Rosie we will be outside for a couple of hours, but we will be close by and check on them."

Peter was halfway down the steps before Ridge finished his sentence.

When he exited the trailer, Peter eagerly poked at the items in the box.

"Let's leave that there for now. Come walk with me and tell me about the setup Karma has in the park for you all, and for the others who live here."

"Most of the others want to be left alone. They tend to stick to their areas of the trailer park and don't help Karma much at all. She rescued most of them, and they haven't figured out how to get away from here on their own yet."

"Some have gotten away?"

Peter tilted his head, thinking. "Some. Karma used to take some to the northern border of the old city limits and help them get across the river. The latest batches, though, don't want much to do with anyone and don't want Karma's help any longer. Well, other than leeching off her. They don't leave the park *ever*." His annoyance rang true in his voice.

"Do they help inside here? Tending to the traps and helping with stuff like taking care of Rosie and Lily?"

"Nope," Peter stated flatly. "Karma keeps them away from us for the most part. Some of them are mad at Karma."

"Why are they angry at Karma?"

"The angry ones are sometimes family of people Karma rescued but couldn't save. I've heard bits of things when Rosie and Karma are talking, thinking that I'm asleep." He shrugged his shoulders sheepishly.

"Grown-up conversations are usually not for younger ears."

"I'm hardly a child!" Peter protested.

"You are barely a teen," Ridge said simply. "You are a huge help. You're getting stronger every day, and you haven't grown up easily, so you are more grown than most others your age would be. But that still doesn't mean you should listen to grown-up conversations."

Peter huffed a bit, but his cheeks reddened.

Changing the subject, Ridge ruffled his hair. "Show me the usual boundaries Karma has for you. I'm sure you aren't supposed to wander all over, especially by yourself."

"Yes, sir."

Peter led him around and chattered on, pointing out the "decoy" trailers kept on the edge of his boundaries. The rundown shells were obviously in rough shape and abandoned, but they were positioned strategically to conceal the nicest parts of the other trailers, which were being used as homes. Most people would look from a distance and assume *all* the trailers in the park were in the same condition—unlivable.

"Do the other trailers have tunnels too?"

"No, sir. Karma dug those specially for us. She wanted to be able to hide Lily and me, especially when we were littler."

Ridge stopped and looked at Peter. "You keep calling me 'sir.' Why?"

"My papa said I should always show respect to people when we first meet. Until they show me they don't deserve it, or until they give me permission to use another name, I am supposed to say 'sir' or 'ma'am.'"

"Peter, you can call me Ridge, okay?"

"Yes, sir."

Ridge laughed and ruffled his hair, continuing down the path. "Peter, did your dad go to Phoenix Corps?"

Peter dipped his head in affirmation. "Karma got him out, and when he told her about me and Mama, she came to find us. Brought us here."

Ridge pretended not to see Peter wipe his eyes with his sleeve. He remained quiet, waiting for him to continue.

"Dad got sick. Sicker than Lily is. He got better for a while. Karma let us stay in the trailer over there." He pointed to a burnt-out shell just past his boundary. "I was still pretty little. Seven, I think. I spilled something on the carpet, and Dad got mad. He never got mad before Phoenix Corps took him. But he kept getting madder and madder."

Peter's eyes went distant, unfocused, storm clouds brewing in their blue depths. He swiped angrily at them again with his sleeve and continued. "Mom tried to calm him down. She got between us. Karma heard her scream when she was coming back from checking traps, grabbed me up, and pulled me out of the trailer. I think Mom was dead before Karma grabbed me, but she went back in. The trailer looked like it was dancing, tipping one way, then the next."

He pointed at a body-sized imprint protruding next to what had probably been the kitchen window.

That dent—it was about the size he'd expect if it had been Karma shoved against the wall. It took more effort than it should to calm the rage racing through his veins.

Peter sat down, facing away from the charred remains, regaining Ridge's attention. "It took forever for the slamming to stop. I heard him shout—madder than I ever heard him before. Something slammed into the ceiling really hard. And then I couldn't hear anything." He closed his eyes. "The light was so bright. And I was sweating from the heat. Karma picked me up and carried me back to her trailer. Her skin. It was the first time I saw it. Touched it. It feels like armor. She put me with Lily and Mrs. Thorn. She didn't have the tunnel finished yet, but she told them to take me to the hidden hallway. Lily and I used old chunks of burned wood, and we drew on the walls for a long time."

"I saw those drawings. Nice job sprucing up that area."

Peter gave him a small, sad smile. "Karma didn't make it back until the next morning. She hugged me and told me she'd take care of me. She smelled like smoke. Like a lot of smoke. I heard her talking to Mrs. Thorn later. Mom died. Dad tried to fight Karma; he wanted to get out to me, but she wouldn't let him. Dad ripped up the stove, and it hit the ceiling. There was still gas for the stove then. Something sparked. Karma made it out." His smile turned sheepish. "If I didn't listen, I'd never know what happened. I think Karma is scared I won't like her if I know. But she did what she said. She takes care of me."

They took a few steps, and Peter looked at him with wide, frightened eyes. "You won't tell her I know, will you?"

"No, buddy." Ridge patted his shoulder. "Though you show her every day how much she means to you. If you let her know you've always known, maybe she won't have to be scared of you finding out, ya know?"

Peter scrunched his brow in concentration, then turned his young face to Ridge. "I'll think about that. You might be right."

Ridge ruffled his hair and ushered him along.

Circuit finished, Ridge entered the hidden cove between the trailers, where the hidden hallway was. The thought put into the placement of the trailers and run-down but intact sheds, with the old trees, hid the hallway perfectly. Even a small space for a clearing was tucked inside.

"If we get a really sunny day, Karma will bring us out here for a picnic. Sometimes for special occasions. She picks a day every year for each of us to celebrate. I don't remember my real birthday. I only know it was sometime in July. So, Karma picks a day to celebrate. Rosie won't tell anyone her birthday." His voice dropped to a conspiratorial whisper. "She's afraid we'll somehow guess how old she is. She says the quake erased birthdays so she could start all over again."

"Do you mind sharing your picnic space with a small garden? It looks like this area gets enough sun, and you guys could have spices to put in your food, like the food I made yesterday."

"And it will be a surprise?"

"Karma doesn't know I'm doing it, so I'm sure she will be surprised," Ridge replied, crossing his fingers that she wouldn't kick his ass for doing it without her approval first.

Chapter 19

Karma

She must have slept for a few hours, because Karma felt mildly refreshed. Annabeth still slept in the other room, but her temperature had dropped closer to normal.

Karma headed for the door to check on the others when Ridge's scent registered, stronger than it should have been with him being gone for hours. She cautiously opened the door and peered outside. She didn't see him, but Peter's scent mingled with his outside.

Karma followed her nose. In the picnic area stood a pile of brick and wood about three feet high. That hadn't been there before. She stepped closer, peering over the edge to find plants inside—herbs, like the ones Ridge used when cooking the meat, if her nose could be believed.

Laughter reached her ears, and she turned, finding Peter walking backward, talking animatedly with Ridge, who carried a still pale Lily. The sight stole her breath.

Ridge's eyes locked onto hers, and a nervous smile turned up his lips.

"Looks like you were busy while I slept this morning."

"I got to help!" Peter shouted excitedly, running to stand next to her. "Do you like it?"

"Lily insisted on coming up to see it, and I figured a little bit of sun wouldn't hurt."

She heard the trepidation in his voice, like he was afraid he'd done something wrong. She couldn't help her smile, but ignored the fluttering in her belly, the warmth blooming in her heart. "I'd planned to bring her out for a bit today, and the garden is a wonderful addition. Thank you."

Peter dropped the picnic blanket he'd carried and spread it out. Ridge lowered Lily to the sunniest spot. "I'll bring Rosie next. Do you want Annabeth out here, too?"

"No."

A quick nod, and he disappeared back around the trailer.

There wasn't time for silence as Peter rattled on about how much Ridge let him do and what he learned. He announced that he would take responsibility for the garden for them. Peter glowed with the attention from Ridge. She couldn't remember a time when he smiled so much. Karma tried to make things as easy for Lily and Peter as she could, but it was hard. Life was hard, and there wasn't a lot of room for the gentleness and innocence of a child. They'd both had to grow up fast, their eyes opened to the dangers and evil much too early.

Peter still talked, the hero worship in his voice evident, as Ridge settled Rosie down next to Lily. His cheeks flushed as he heard Peter's praises.

"Just remember the watering schedule I told you about. That's the most important part with these plants."

Peter nodded. "I will do it exactly how you showed me."

Ridge took a seat next to her. His muscular thigh pressed against hers. A broad shoulder just behind hers, tempting her to lean against it.

The conversation flowed, but Karma barely heard a word of it. Ridge consumed her senses. The hardness of his muscles, the warmth of his body, the spicy musk of his scent, the low rumble of his voice settled into her core, curling her toes. Memories of the dreams haunting her since she'd met him flooded her mind, the vivid, green eyes in the dark of the buildings from their first encounter. His protectiveness when helping her with Pip. His powerful muscles as he held her against him, hiding her from the goon squad. The softness of his skin over the flexible steel of his muscles as she worked to keep him cool during his infection. The power he exuded with his kiss had nearly dropped her to her knees, and the patience and caring he showed to Lily, Peter, and Rosie, people he had *no* responsibility for.

"You feeling okay, Karma?" Rosie asked. "You're a bit flushed."

Karma sat up straighter and shifted so she wasn't touching Ridge and cleared her throat. Her voice was still husky when she said, "Fine. Just tired." She needed to shake off this reaction to him. It couldn't go anywhere. She had a mission—destroy Phoenix Corp. Distractions could be deadly.

"I need to go check on Annabeth."

"I'll get Lily and Rosie back inside to rest." Ridge stood too, resting his hand on the small of her back.

Karma stepped forward, removing his touch, and caught the smirk on his face out of the corner of her eye.

Annabeth was up and moving, coming back from the bathroom. Her shoulders hunched, and she sat down hard on the old couch.

"I'm glad to see you able to get up on your own," Karma said, pulling out a can of soup. "I'll get you something to eat, and then you should rest some more. Your fever will likely return again tonight."

Annabeth huffed and puffed, out of breath just from her short walk to the bathroom and back. "I appreciate you helping me."

"No one deserves the treatment Phoenix Corps gives."

"How many other people are here in your trailer?" she asked.

"You and me."

"Where's Lily?"

"In her trailer."

"That's it? I thought I remembered someone else."

"Ridge. He's..."

"A friend," Ridge finished, coming into the trailer and stopping next to Karma, his hand on the small of her back and a glint of humor and mischief in those green eyes of his.

"That's it? Just you two?" Annabeth turned her attention back to Karma, having been drawn to Ridge since he'd entered. "How many people have you gotten out of Phoenix Corps?"

"A few," Karma answered simply. "I've helped people out and helped them get out of the area, out of Phoenix Corps's reach."

"How many?"

"Well, there's you and Lily, Jacob and Judy. Your father. I've helped most of the people still living here in the trailer park. A few others that I helped escape Fairway entirely," Karma answered, then poured the warmed soup into a can. She pushed past Ridge, slipping him another unopened can, Annabeth's view blocked by Karma's body, and then handed Annabeth the can and spoon.

"I've got a few errands. I'll be back in a bit to check on you." Ridge left the trailer, whistling. His whistle faded off as he walked in the direction of Mrs. Thorn's trailer.

Karma refocused on Annabeth. "Eat up, and I'll get you back into bed. Your body is fighting, and it needs rest."

"You won't tie me down again?" she asked, terror in her eyes. "I saw the ropes lying around the bed."

"You were thrashing really hard during some of your fevers. I only tied you down for your safety and to keep you from flinging off the wet rags and mud that were helping to lower your temperature. I've left the ropes there in case you start thrashing again, but as long as your body rests peacefully, I won't tie you up."

She nodded once, then took a bite of the soup.

Once done, Karma helped a weak Annabeth into bed, taking most of her weight. She waited until Annabeth was asleep, then headed back out and around to the other trailer, unsurprised to find Ridge and Peter sitting on the steps.

Ridge whispered something in Peter's ear, ruffled his hair, and patted his shoulder. Peter got up and headed back inside. Ridge's intense green eyes met hers. "She's got lots of questions." He pointed over to her trailer. "You don't tell any of them about the others you have here?"

"Beyond who they already know, no. She's probably seen Peter here and there, but they've not interacted. She has run into Lily when Lily has been out checking the traps, so they know each other. Rosie rarely leaves the tunnel anymore. I learned quickly that it is safer for everyone to provide less information. The ones who go mad..." she trailed off, kicking at a stone sticking out of the ground. "The ones who don't recover from what Phoenix Corps did to them, it sometimes can take months to manifest. I've brought families here to reunite, only to have it go terribly wrong a few months later. I may be overly cautious, but I found it works better this way."

The understanding and compassion in Ridge's eyes brought tears to her own. She shook her head and rolled her shoulders, clearing her throat.

"I keep Lily, Peter, and Rosie close. Only you have ever seen where they stay. No one else goes into Mrs. Thorn's old trailer. Once I get people out, most want to leave or seclude themselves, and I won't compromise their security. They've been through enough already."

"I'm honored you allowed me into the inner circle."

"It became a necessity." She hurried to add, "If you betray my trust, I'll string your entrails like fairy lights."

Chapter 20

7619

Ridge

"String my entrails like fairy lights?" he asked, failing to hide his chuckle.

Her fierce protection of those she loved endeared her even further to him. And, he hadn't missed the scent of arousal when they sat in the picnic area. This wasn't one-sided.

Ridge stood and closed the distance between them, continuing forward even as she backed up. Karma was forced to stop when her back hit one of the trees in front of the trailer, and he caged her in with his body again. He laid his hand gently against her throat, feeling her pulse race beneath it. He bent, his lips a whisper from hers, and stifled a smile at the quick intake of her breath. "I promise, I won't cause a problem." He sealed his promise with a kiss, reveling in the way she melted against him. He swallowed her whimpers of need and pressed her tighter to the tree.

The moment she started to stiffen, he backed off, but only enough to put space between their lips. "I'd like to help you." Roughness rode his voice, and he cleared his throat.

Her hackles raised, and she shoved him away from her. "I don't *need* your help."

Ridge gripped her upper arm as she tried to move around him, to escape. "I get that you don't *need* me," he said, emphasizing the word just like she did. "I want to help. I like Peter, Lily, and Rosie. It should be quite obvious that I like you, too. I think I can help. I want to."

Ridge released the hold she hadn't fought and gave her a cocky grin. "I'll see you around." He strode off, leaving the trailer park and heading to check traps along the way back to his hidey hole. It wasn't home. It was just where he spent his nights.

He headed back to the trailer park as the first rays of weak light were peeking over the horizon. Ridge carried an extra mattress, and he picked up a few rats from the traps on the way, taking a circuitous route.

About four blocks from the trailer park, he picked up the scents of some goon squad members he had the misfortune to know; their scents were fresh. Ridge tucked the mattress into a crevice of the one wall left of the old barber shop and bolted into the old laundromat next door. The plumbing in the walls strengthened the structure, leaving three of the four walls still standing. As quietly as he could, Ridge climbed to the top of the second tier of appliances and lay across the top, peering over the top of the wall into the alley. The ceiling and roof of this laundromat collapsed years before, leaving a clear view from above the appliances to the surrounding streets.

Indistinct mumbles, scuffles of feet, and the kicking of debris. They weren't trying to be quiet. He listened as the voices and noises trailed off, away from the park, and waited for ten minutes of silence before lowering himself from his perch and retrieving the mattress.

It was nearing lunchtime when he finally arrived at Karma's trailer, coming in from the opposite end he usually did.

Ridge set the mattress in the hidden picnic cove, then followed Karma's strongest scent. He'd find her in Mrs. Thorn's trailer.

Karma stood at the sink in the kitchen, seemingly lost in thought. He could see her face through the window; she worried the edge of her bottom lip between her teeth.

Ridge knocked quietly so he didn't startle her and tried to push away the thoughts in his head, thoughts he knew she would run from.

Karma watched him warily as she pulled the door open.

"How is Lily today?" he asked.

"Better. Her fever didn't get as high last night. I hope she is pulling through the other side of it."

He placed a comforting hand against her upper arm, but didn't pursue when she pulled away.

"And the others?"

"They are fine. Annabeth didn't seem to have as much trouble last night either."

"So, you got some sleep?"

She shook her head. "I stayed up to watch over them. I didn't want to miss a fever starting." Karma wiped at an already clean spot on the counter.

Ridge stifled a smile. "And is Annabeth still sleeping?"

"She slept restlessly last night, even without such a high fever. I think she really settled in around dawn. I left her to make food for these guys."

"I brought you something."

Karma raised her eyebrow at him. "You already brought us spices."

"Come see it and tell me where you want it." He motioned her through the door ahead of him and was shocked when she didn't hesitate. She *was* starting to trust him more. He wiped the cocky grin off his face before she saw it and placed his hand at the small of her back, guiding her back to the picnic area. "I helped ruin the mattress you have on the cot in your trailer. It's only fair I replace it."

"That's not necessary..."

Ridge took her hand, giving a slight tug, stopping her argument, and bringing her flush to his body. "No arguments. I have a few extra stashed at my place, just in case. I won't miss this one." His voice was soft when he spoke. "Please don't argue. Just tell me where you want me to put it." He dropped a chaste kiss into her hair and waited while she took steady gulps of air.

"Put it in the second bedroom in Mrs. Thorn's trailer for now. I don't want to risk ruining it when Annabeth's fever spikes again." She rose up on her tiptoes and pressed her lips to his cheek. "Thank you, Ridge."

He fought his body's reaction, wanting to turn his head and capture her lips, knowing she'd balk. He couldn't stop the tightening of his arms, pulling her more snugly against him, relishing in the feel of her curves.

"Ridge!"

Peter's excited voice had her pulling away from him, stepping back several paces, and a sweet, pink tinge rising to her cheeks.

He hid his smile as he turned to face Peter's exuberant face.

"It's time to water the spices, right?" Peter practically vibrated out of his shoes.

"Indeed, it is. But first, I need your big, strong arms to help me out." Ridge pointed to the mattress. "Go make sure Rosie and Lily aren't up in the trailer, and then come out and help me carry this heavy mattress in."

Peter gave him a salute and spun back in the direction he came from.

"He really worships you."

While there was some awe in her voice, he detected a hint of worry as well.

"I won't do anything to hurt him," he assured her.

"You won't survive it if you do," she warned, her matter-of-fact, stubborn, and protective side showing.

He only had time to rest his hand along her cheek, his thumb grazing the corner of her mouth, causing the sweet gasp he anticipated, before Peter came rip-roaring around the corner again, ready to help.

Karma stepped back out of reach. "You boys stay out of trouble. I need to check on Annabeth."

Ridge didn't miss the huskiness in her voice and bit his cheek to hide his smile.

Chapter 21

Karma

Karma pressed her back against the trailer door as she closed it, attempting to calm her racing heart. She needed to stop reacting to Ridge in this way. He'd never stick around. She'd *never* depend on someone else again. It was up to her to keep Peter, Lily, and Rosie safe. To take down Phoenix Corps. To somehow stop the madness that had taken over their world.

Annabeth was coming down the hall from the bathroom, her shoulders hunched forward and her feet sliding over the worn flooring, as if they were too heavy to lift.

Karma rushed to her aid, taking most of her weight as she put her arm around her, leading her back to the cot.

Sitting Annabeth in the chair next to the cot, Karma changed the bedding she kept between Annabeth and the mattress, trying to save her from the worst of the substances ruining the mattress.

Once she had Annabeth back in bed, Karma heated some more food from her stores, noting how low it was getting in the cabinets, and took her the meager meal.

Her first opportunity, she'd check the supplies in the tunnel and check on her traps. Exhaustion pulled at her from her late nights and worry. Karma lay down hard on the lumpy, rough sofa and drifted into oblivion, unable to stop the pull.

The strange orangish light from the setting sun peeked into the kitchen window when Karma opened her eyes. She listened, unmoving, for the sound that woke her. When she heard it again, she was on her feet, rushing to the bedroom where Annabeth lay whimpering in her sleep.

Karma touched her forehead and found it warm, but not blazing hot.

Annabeth's brow wrinkled at the contact, and her hand struck out with incredible speed, gripping Karma's wrist in a vise. Her unseeing eyes opened, her pupils elongated from top to bottom, and locked on something over Karma's shoulder. Her mouth opened in a silent scream, and in front of Annabeth's canines, two needle-like fangs dropped.

Karma jammed her other hand against Annabeth's forehead, keeping her pressed against the mattress so she couldn't reach Karma's arm to bite with those fangs.

"Annabeth," Karma said calmly, attempting to pry her wrist from Annabeth's vise-like hold without hurting her. "Annabeth, you are safe here."

It took more effort than Karma thought it would to remove her wrist, leaving behind an already purpling bruise and raw, reddened skin. Karma grabbed the rope again, securing Annabeth's arms and feet, despite the continued thrashing. She searched Annabeth's arms and legs, looking for any recent cuts that could show where a tracker had been implanted or one of their tattoos. But she found nothing.

Sweating from the effort and needing air, Karma pushed out into the cool night, pulling in deep gulps of the refreshing air. Panic threatened to choke her. Annabeth shouldn't have *any* of these traits after just one injection. Phoenix Corps must have really improved their serums. Lily hadn't shown any signs of this kind of change.

She stumbled in her race to get around to Mrs. Thorn's trailer and barreled in the door, nearly falling on Ridge, who stood in the kitchen happily chatting with Peter.

In an instant, his eyes took her in from head to toe. Ridge backed her up and made a motion with his hand to Peter, who disappeared into the trap door.

He ushered her over to the chair Peter had vacated and pushed her gently into it, holding her there with his hand on her shoulder when she tried to get back up.

"What happened?" he asked, his voice held barely restrained rage.

"I didn't find a tracker. Or a tattoo."

Ridge's demeanor changed in the blink of an eye. One moment, his demeanor was gentle and coaxing, despite the fury that lay beneath it. The next, he'd spun on his heel, in fighting stance, ready to take on anything that came through the door. "Where are they?" The rumble in his voice made her thankful she was sitting; her knees would've melted otherwise.

She reached her hand up, laying it at the small of his back, feeling the muscles there coiled and ready to spring into action at a moment's notice. "I haven't seen anyone. I didn't mean to panic you, too. There's no immediate threat." She shook her head in defeat and shame. "But I was stupid and careless. I just... damnit!"

His green eyes turned back to her. She didn't want to put a name to what she saw there. "What happened?"

"Annabeth was dreaming—maybe a low fever now, but nothing like before. I tried to reassure her that she was safe. She was lightning fast and strong. She had fangs, and her pupils were unusually shaped. She should have a tracker and a tattoo if she's this far in. I didn't find *any*." She lowered her gaze again, shame and guilt threatening to choke her. "If I missed them somehow. Lily, Peter, and Rosie..."

Ridge lifted her chin, making her meet his eyes. "We won't let anything happen to them. I can take them to my place for a while, if you want." His hand drifted from her shoulder, down her arm, and abruptly stopped when it reached the visible bruising. Rage once again swirled in the depths of his eyes. "You're coming, too."

Karma stiffened at the command. She shoved him away and stood, her panic morphing into anger. "I screwed up. I've put them in danger. I appreciate you offering to keep them safe at your place. But don't for one damn minute think you get to order me around. I made the mistake. But I refuse to lose what I've built here."

Ridge grabbed her forearm, lifting it to eye level, forcing her to see the extent of the bruising. "She needs to go. Now. And no one said you had to leave forever. But it's no safer for you here than for the others."

Karma shoved him, dislodging his grip. "I'll help you get them to your place. Tonight. I'll bring you extra supplies when I can. I'll make it safe for them to return as soon as I can." Karma forced her way past him, making her way into the tunnel.

Within fifteen minutes, they'd packed up some supplies and headed out of the trailer park. Ridge carried Rosie despite her protests, Karma carried the supplies and took the lead, watching for anything out of the ordinary as they made their way through the streets as darkness descended. Peter and Lily walked behind Karma, with Peter helping Lily as she started to tire out.

By the time she was ready to head back to the trailer, full dark had fallen. Ridge escorted her to the edge of his building, stopping her with a gentle hand on her shoulder.

"I'll check traps tomorrow morning and bring you what I can," she rushed to say before he could speak.

"Karma, stop." He tugged on her shoulder, trying to get her to turn around.

When she refused, he stepped in front of her, forcing her to look at him.

"Stay here," he pleaded. "If it's not safe back there."

"Annabeth still needs help. Thank you for keeping Lily, Peter, and Rosie safe."

"I'll keep them safe. I want to keep *you* safe, too."

She bit her lip to stave off the tears threatening at his words and the softness in his eyes.

His full lips crashed down on hers, pulling her flush with his body. The hard ridges of muscle against her softer curves sent tingles along her nerve endings. He swallowed her moan and shifted the angle, deepening the kiss, turning her legs to jelly.

Her fists bunched in his shirt, the fabric abrading her skin in the most delicious way. His warmth penetrated the fabric and seeped into her hands and bare arms, warming her through her own clothes, tempting her to stay within his cocoon.

He pulled back from the kiss too soon, but not soon enough.

Her mind warred with her body and heart, and she spun on her heel, dislodging herself from his embrace.

His hand rested lightly on her shoulder, stopping her from running away. He stepped up behind her, the heat of his body searing her from behind. "I'll keep them safe, Karma," he repeated, his gruff voice scraping over her already overly sensitive nerves.

Her breath shuddered at the sensation, and she stepped out of his reach again.

Ridge let his hand fall to his side. "I'll check on you soon."

"Stay with them, please." She hated the pleading she heard in her own voice as she walked away.

Chapter 22

Ridge

Karma's retreating form left her intoxicating scent in her wake. He itched to follow it, follow her back, and make sure she was safe.

She was stubborn, he'd give her that, but he was determined to wear her down. Whatever was holding her back from him was an obstacle he had to overcome, and he would.

When he could no longer see her or hear her steps, Ridge turned and went back down into his hidey hole with the others. Rosie had been quiet, and Lily needed rest. Peter kept himself busy, bringing them water and food and helping them to settle in while Ridge had been on the surface with Karma.

He bounded over, bouncing on his feet with excitement. "It's been a long time since I got to leave the trailer park! This is great! But why are we here? Where did Karma go? Isn't she staying too?"

Ridge bent to his level, resting his hand on Peter's shoulder to keep him from bouncing. "Karma is taking care of Annabeth right now, remember. She went back to take care of her."

Peter's bottom lip puffed out. "She's not taking care of us anymore?"

"No, that's not it, bud." Ridge tucked Peter under his arm. "Annabeth is stronger than we thought, and we want to make sure you guys are safe. The best way for us to do that is for you to come and hang out with me for a bit. Sound good?"

Peter's head dipped in agreement, but there was a sadness in his posture Ridge couldn't ignore.

"I'm gonna need your help with these girls," he whispered conspiratorially. "And I'll take you with me to tend my spices, so you can get more practice."

His eyes lit with excitement for a split second, then sobered again. "What about our garden?"

"You don't think I'd let the plants die after all the work we did to get them going, do you?"

Peter's shrug caused a pang in Ridge's heart.

"I know it won't be the same, tending to my garden, but Karma is going to do everything she can to get you back to the trailers as soon as it is safe."

"What about her? Is she safe?"

"She's a strong lady. But don't worry. I'm keeping my eye on her, too."

Peter abruptly threw his arms around Ridge's chest and squeezed tight. "Thank you," he whispered. "She needs someone looking out for *her*."

Ridge tossed and turned through the night. If it wasn't worry for Karma keeping him up, it was the strange sounds of others in his space—something he would need to get used to. He knew he needed to give Karma some space, stop pawing her every time they were together, but he wasn't quite sure how he would manage it.

He raced to the trapdoor before the weak dawn light touched it, hearing soft steps on the floorboards above. Whoever it was managed to be very quiet, but there was no hiding their scent. His adrenaline spiked, and his blood raced, but he held tight to his leash of control and quietly lifted the door.

Karma startled at his appearance and jumped back, nearly falling over a piece of debris on the ground.

Ridge grabbed her hand, stopping her fall, pulling her against him. The moment he was sure she'd regained her balance, he stepped away, giving her breathing room, even though every instinct he had told him to keep her there.

He traced her body with his eyes, checking for any sign of injury. Eyes landing on the bruise on her wrist, vivid even in the dim light of the dawn, his gut clenched at the sight. He should've been there, should've stopped it. His gaze dropped lower, and he saw why she'd come.

Four rats hung from her fingers by their tails. She held them out to him uncertainly.

Ridge was careful not to touch her hand when he took them from her. "How is your patient this morning?"

"She says she doesn't remember any dreams from last night. Her eyes are back to normal, and her fangs are gone."

"It won't stay that way."

"I know," she said sadly.

"Did you leave her tied up?" Karma shook her head, and Ridge clenched his jaw. "You should stay to say hi to Peter. He was afraid you weren't going to take care of them anymore, that you were giving that responsibility to me."

For a fragment of time, anguish showed on her face. In the blink of an eye, her face cleared, and she visibly steeled her spine. "This is just temporary." Anger laced her tone.

Ridge raised his hands in surrender. "I know that. You know that. He's scared to be without you." He waved the rats, "I'll cook breakfast. You visit."

"I can only stay for a bit. I need to get back to Annabeth."

Before she could descend into his space, he stopped her with a light touch on the silky skin of her cheek, "When I went to the trailer park yesterday, a few blocks away, I heard a couple of members of the goon squad I recognized. Don't know what they were talking about, but make sure you are extra vigilant when you are moving around out there. Okay?"

She didn't respond except for a twitch of her jaw and a softening in her eyes. Karma descended into the darkness of his space, and he heard Peter exclaim and bound over to her by the time she reached the floor.

Karma was quiet through breakfast. She smiled as Peter talked incessantly, but it never quite reached her eyes, and her eyes kept straying to Lily.

Ridge focused on her covertly, taking in the dark circles visible even in the dim light around the small table. Her shoulders sagged as if the weight of the world rested on them. She ate, but not enough to sustain her, pushing more of her food onto Lily's and Peter's plates.

He set Peter and Lily to the task of cleaning up the meal and headed to the surface with Karma. "She's fine," he said, stopping her with a hand on her unbruised wrist. "Lily, I mean. There was barely a fever last night. I think she's coming out the other side now."

"Good," Karma replied absently, her eyes locked onto the fingers still wrapped around her wrist.

"I can check some of the traps later, bring food to you tonight."

She shook her head no. "Stay with them. Keep them safe."

"You need rest, Karma. You will be no good to Lily and Peter if you don't start taking care of yourself."

Fire blazed hot in her eyes, and she lifted her glare to his face. "I asked you to take care of *them*. Not me." Karma spun on her heel and trudged off toward the trailer park.

"Oh, I plan to do both," he murmured to her retreating back.

Ridge used an old, rusted screwdriver, the only one he had, to remove handles and locks from two doors in the shell of a building a few blocks from his hidey-hole. Peter stood over his shoulder, watching him with avid interest, taking in each move he made and asking questions, trying to keep his voice down despite the excitement buzzing through him.

"What are you going to do with these after you take them off?" he whispered, pointing at the doors.

"Not using the doors for anything. I'm going to take the handles and locks. The ones at the trailer park are too flimsy and easily broken or picked. I want to make sure when you guys go back to the trailer, that you stay safe."

"So, we are going to go back?" Peter asked, timidity rode his voice.

"Yes. Karma only wants you to stay here until she is sure it is safe for you to come back."

"Are you coming back with us?"

Ridge was surprised by how much he wanted to say yes. Sure, he was attracted to Karma, but she represented a family. Even if it wasn't truly her blood family, these kids were as much hers as if she'd birthed them.

He'd been alone almost all his life. Before Phoenix Corps, he'd had a girl on his arm anytime he wanted one. But they were never going to be there for the long haul. Karma, he couldn't say that about. She'd go to the ends of the earth for the people she loved. And he found he wanted to go to the ends of the earth for *her*. The thought scared him.

He'd been on his own for decades before Phoenix Corps, and since then, he trusted no one. But, since their first encounter, he'd been fascinated by Karma. And he trusted her. She'd helped get him away from Phoenix Corps. She'd nursed him back to health twice since. And she left the things most precious to her in his care, trusting him.

He'd briefly encountered a lot of people both before and after Phoenix Corps. Never once did he want to keep them around. Karma was different.

"I don't plan on disappearing from your life any time soon," Ridge managed to say around the ball of swirling emotions lodged in his throat. "Hand me that knife carefully."

Ridge pried the old lock free from the weather-swollen wood and tucked it into the box with his tools. He and Peter gathered some spices, and they returned to check on Lily and Rosie.

He tucked Peter back inside with the women, leaving them with instructions to be quiet and remain inside. Then he headed back to the trailer park. He caught the scents of the owners of the voices he'd heard the day before.

Ridge trailed the perimeter of the area but couldn't make sense of the directions any of them had come from or which direction they headed back out. He altered his path, crisscrossing and backtracking so he couldn't be followed, then headed straight for Mrs. Thorn's old trailer.

The brass door handle and lock in his hand were tarnished from weather exposure, but even in that condition, it was better security than the current setup on the trailer doors. He worked quietly, replacing the handle on Mrs. Thorn's trailer before heading to Karma's.

Chapter 23

5713

Karma

A quiet jiggle on the trailer's door handle had her on her feet. Karma flattened herself against the wall beside the door, knife ready.

Spice and musk wafted in as the door cracked open the slightest amount before being pulled back tight.

"Ridge?" Karma whispered.

"Yeah, it's me. Sorry, didn't mean to startle you." His voice was muffled through the door. He pushed it back open again. "I'd hoped you were sleeping, and I planned to be done and gone before you were awake."

"What are you doing?"

"Changing out your door handles. The ones you currently have are too easy to pick or just break. These will at least give you a few extra seconds to get prepared or hide if someone you won't want to show up does."

"Like you? Showing up when you should be *far from here.*"

"Everything is fine back at my place. I wouldn't be here unless I was sure."

Karma looked at the bed where Annabeth lay, then back at Ridge.

His brow furrowed a bit, then he stepped back, allowing her to descend the stairs and join him outside. "What is it?" he asked, keeping his voice quiet and stepping away from the door, his warm hand on the small of her back, guiding her away from the trailer.

"Annabeth's fevers haven't been spiking, but since she is so far into the altering process, she should've been back on her feet already."

"What about the others you've helped?"

"Phoenix Corps is improving their methods. Things are happening faster than ever before when it comes to altering. Those I've helped who were fully altered or close...their animals have healed them.

They'd have been out the door and onto their own lives by now." She stepped forward, away from the maddening sensations his hand on her back and rubbing slow circles with his thumb caused.

Ridge clenched his hand, as if keeping himself from reaching for her again.

Karma took another step away, against her every instinct screaming at her to get closer.

He leaned against the trunk of a tree in the yard, his posture casual, but the look in his eye was alert and razor sharp. "I don't like you staying here alone with her. Especially knowing she is so far into the process that she has fangs."

She bristled. "I can take care of myself."

"Never said you couldn't. I would just prefer if you didn't have to." Ridge walked away from the tree but still kept his distance. "Do you know what her animal is? Has she said anything about it?"

"No. Short of a tattoo or peeling away some of her flesh to the animal hide beneath, I can only guess. And she hasn't spoken much. She spends most of her time sleeping. She gets up and uses the bathroom on her own, but I usually have to help her get back down the hall and into bed."

"Still?"

"She's that weak when she comes out, yes."

"She shouldn't still be..."

"I know." Karma plopped onto the ground. Her feet wanted to carry her back to him, within his reach, so she could soak up the comfort and support she desperately wanted, and she couldn't allow that weakness.

"What is your best guess for her animal?"

"Snake." She shook her head before he could ask. "I don't know what kind. I assume something poisonous because it's Phoenix Corps. The fangs and eyes match. Her skin is cooler when she's not feverish, similar to mine. I won't skin her to find out for sure—not that I could tell just from scales anyhow."

"What happens next?"

"Hopefully, she gets her strength back soon, and she can get away from here. Otherwise, I don't know."

"If she wants to stay?"

"No one here is fully altered. I'm it. They run to stay out of Phoenix Corps' hands." Karma pulled absently at the grass. "They figured out early that the 'treatments' they use must be administered on a schedule. If too much time passes between one treatment and the next, the human body's immune system builds up against whatever they are injecting. The process halts completely, and full Altered status is impossible—one of the many reasons they get so cranky when someone escapes."

"Do you think she is fully altered?"

"I wouldn't be surprised."

"What can I do to help?"

"Go home. Tend to your responsibilities there," she said pointedly.

"I caught the scent of the goon squad again. Or at least people who are using the masking soap from Phoenix Corps. They were in the same general area again, near the laundromat."

"I'll steer clear of that area."

"Karma..." Ridge started.

"Go home, Ridge." Karma dug her nails into the skin of her palm, leaving pain and marks in their wake. "Please." She hated the plea in her voice, but she couldn't afford to let her guard down.

Ridge opened his mouth, like he would argue, and she looked away. If he asked her again to stay, she might not have the strength to tell him no. His voice was quiet when he spoke, "I'll go. But I'm finishing your new door handle first."

Karma went back in the trailer and, after checking on Annabeth, sat on the couch as Ridge worked on replacing the door handle and bolt lock. His muscles bunched as he moved, stretching the soft fabric of his t-shirt. She picked up her weaving, trying to distract herself, but kept having to tear the stitches back out because she was paying more attention to Ridge than to what she was *supposed* to be working on.

Ridge unfolded to his full height, tucking the tools into his back pocket, turning to her. "Lock up when I leave." He looked like he wanted to say more. Instead, he turned and walked away.

Karma slammed the new deadbolt home, keeping herself locked in the trailer and not running after him like she so desperately wanted.

Chapter 24

Ridge

Frustration and sadness engulfed him as he walked back to his hidey hole. He tried to shake it off, knowing he couldn't be alone in his space to deal with it, but Karma twisted him up in knots. She refused to be vulnerable with him. And he understood why. Hell, he'd lived the why, but that didn't make his frustration any better.

Even outside, the wind seemed determined to bring her scent closer, surround him with it. His palms itched to reach for her. To take her burdens. To hold her close and protect her as she'd done for so many people for so long.

He picked up a big hunk of brick and chucked it down the alley, listening to it crash and ping off walls, exposed pipes, and metal. It didn't improve his mood any.

Ridge was still grumbling when he reached his trap-door.

He descended into the darkness where the whispers reached his ears. Lily, Peter, and Rosie sat in the corner of the room playing a game of cards.

Lily put her cards down and stood, striding up to him. "Sit down and play. Let me get dinner tonight, please?"

He forced a smile and nodded at her, patting her shoulder as she walked past him to where he kept his food stores. Ridge sat down, picking up Lily's cards, staring at them unseeing. His mind swirled—Karma's scent still lingered here, on the kids and Rosie, on him.

Rosie reached for his hand and squeezed. "Peter, why don't you go and help Lily get some dinner ready for us?"

Peter jumped to his feet and raced across the dimly lit room to help.

"What's the matter, Ridge?" Rosie prodded. She coughed roughly. It rattled her whole frame.

"Do you need some water?"

"Don't worry about this old woman. What's wrong? Are we overstaying our welcome?"

"No!" he said sharply. At her dubious look, he continued, "No, having people here is something I need to get used to, yes. But that has nothing to do with my mood. I'm sorry if I made it seem that way."

"Karma?" she asked secretively, with a wink. His face must have given her the answer she was looking for because she laughed and patted his hand with her spindly fingers. "She's a tough one. Been on her own a long time. Longer than she realizes. I've seen the way she looks at you. The way you look at her, too. Give her time, Ridge. Be persistent but give her time. She notices the little things you've been doing. Caring for us. The little garden. The locks for the door Peter raved about this afternoon. She's worried right now. That will take all her focus for a while, but she still sees what you are doing. Keep doing it. Make her see she can count on you. Don't shy away from the hard stuff."

Ridge blinked at her. While her body might be frail, Rosie's mind was not.

"I want to help her. She just keeps pushing me away."

Rosie gathered up the cards, absently stacking them. "She's a tough nut to crack, our Karma. She's had to be. She doesn't trust easily. Yes, she takes care of all the people in the trailer park, ensuring they have food and supplies, and visits with them to keep them company, if they want. She even makes little improvements to the trailers when she finds supplies. But she doesn't allow them access to us. No one knows about the tunnel or the hidden hallway. She won't take the chance that Phoenix Corps will take one of them and compromise our safety." Her eyes trailed off in thought.

He waited for her to continue.

"There are those who hold resentment against her because she didn't rescue them fast enough, didn't save their loved one in time. They want the stability she provides, but they hate her for it, too. And she's let you in. She knows deep down that she can trust you. You wouldn't have access to us if she didn't. She'll soon come to that realization, too. I have faith in you. I can tell. You're a good egg."

Ridge dropped his eyes. "I'm not a good egg. I've done things."

"Oh, honey, we've all done things, especially since the quake. But I can tell. I've seen a lot in my years. You and Karma are cut from the same cloth. She does everything for everyone else first. She always comes last."

"I don't take care of people like she does," Ridge said, confused. "I've done everything possible to be solitary since I escaped."

Rosie struggled to her feet and bent, pressing a light kiss to his hair. "Yet, since you met Karma and us, you've helped every step of the way—even when she tells you to stop." She winked at him. "How many meals have you taken less because you gave Peter, or Lily, or me extra? I've seen you give Karma extra, too.

Ridge shrugged. "You aren't just some random person on the street."

"Karma and Lily were just random people on the street when you ran into them the first time."

"Still..."

"You're running out of arguments, son. Just accept it. You *are* a good egg. Karma never would've allowed you anywhere near those kids or me if you weren't." Rosie grabbed onto his shoulder as another cough wracked her body. "I'm glad they have you. It'll bring me peace, knowing you will help to protect them all." Her voice was quiet, only loud enough for his enhanced hearing to catch.

"Can we get you medicine? Find a doctor?"

"I'm an old woman. Even if there was a doctor around that wasn't one of Phoenix Corps' mad scientists, they couldn't help me." She squeezed his shoulder. "Knowing I'm not leaving them alone makes it easier."

Ridge bit the inside of his cheek to stem the tears burning his eyes.

Rosie didn't deserve to suffer in this world they were left with. The harsh realities that stole innocence from children and destroyed families. Phoenix Corps capitalized on desperation and vulnerabilities, exploiting everyone.

In the short time he'd known them, Ridge realized he'd come to care for them. Not just Karma, but *all* of them. Peter's enthusiasm and curiosity made him smile. Lily, while still a child herself, was tough, like Karma. Rosie's grandmotherly love and compassion were rare qualities in today's world. And Karma—well, Karma's haunting eyes threatened to drown him. He admired her courage and selflessness. Her beauty drew him in, not just her physical beauty, but the beauty within called to him. Made him want to be better, to help her fight for the future they all deserved, not the future they were headed for.

Chapter 25

5713

Karma

It was still dark, and the air chilled her skin when Karma started out of the trailer park, heading to Ridge's. Small creatures skittered into hiding places as she walked by. Old scents prickled her nose. As she passed the laundromat, the faint odor of the masking soaps used in Phoenix Corps reached her. A faint, familiar smell mingled with the masked scents and tickled her senses, but she couldn't place it. She filed it away and slinked off into the darkness of the next alley.

Ridge sat on a partial wall at the corner of his home, so lost in thought she was within arm's reach before he reacted.

She backed out of his reach with her hands raised. "Sorry, thought you'd have heard me come up."

He blew out a harsh breath. "No, I'm sorry. I shouldn't have gotten so caught up in my head that I didn't notice what was around me. It was stupid."

"You're human."

He scoffed.

"Despite what Phoenix Corps did to us, we *are* still human, Ridge."

"They're starting to move around down there. Go ahead down and see them."

As she headed into the basement, she tried to dissect the sadness she heard in his tone. Maybe he didn't like having the others here. She'd have to figure out another solution soon.

Peter's excited voice reached her a moment before he wrapped his arms around her in a bear hug, telling her all about how he'd been helping Ridge with the door locks and his garden.

Lily stood back, waiting for her turn to hug Karma, then grabbed him by the shirt sleeve and pulled him up and out of the trap door.

The sound of labored breathing reached her ears, and she hurried over to the cot Rosie lay on.

"Don't fuss over me now, Karma. You save it for those kids. You hear me?" Rosie scolded.

Karma tried to help her into a more upright position, but Rosie waved her away.

"Later. For now, sit here and listen to me."

Rosie's ragged breathing tugged hard at her heart.

"Talk to me about him." Rosie's eyes drifted to the now closed trap door.

"What about him?"

"Don't act dumb. My time is limited, and I don't want to dance around the topic."

"I don't..."

Rosie gripped Karma's hand in a surprisingly strong grip, interrupting her. "That man up there is willing and wanting to help you. Let him, Karma. It's time to see some beauty in this dreary world."

"He's not staying, Rosie."

"Bullshit. You're scared. It is understandable. But him leaving? That's bullshit and you know it."

Karma tried to wave away her words.

"Listen to me, child. He's a good one. I see the way he looks at you. The way you look at him when you think no one is watching. The way he treats me and the kids. He's not going to run when it gets hard."

The pleading in her voice tugged at Karma's heart. She heard the truth in Rosie's words; the truth she knew Rosie believed. But she wasn't so sure she believed it. She wanted to, yes, but opening herself up to heartbreak again... No, Karma wasn't ready for that; she might never be.

"I hear your gears turning. You are trying to deny what you want, to protect your heart. If there is one thing I've learned in the many years I've been on this earth, especially since the quake, it's that you need to find the beauty and capture it, hold on to it. It is few and far between, especially now. You'll only hurt yourself in the long run if you continue to run away from the opportunity in front of you. Let him help you. Let him take some of the burden from you."

"Who says he wants that?"

"You can be so stubborn at times. I know you've had to be all of your life, but right now, you are letting it hold you back."

"What are you talking about?"

"Karma, when you set your mind to something, it will get done, no matter the time it takes or the things it costs you. You had to be that way with

Dorian. If it hadn't been for you pushing him to be better, pushing him to get things done, that man would've been content to float through life. "

"That's not true. He worked hard and pushed himself."

"Honey," Rosie grabbed her hand, squeezed lightly, and continued, "You and I both know that he didn't go off to sign up out of the goodness of his heart to help people. He did it so you wouldn't. So, he wouldn't look or feel weak, because you were willing to do something he wouldn't. He wanted to appear to everyone as a strong husband, but it was always you taking care of everything and allowing him to take credit for it. You've romanticized that man since before you married him. He wanted to make you smile. Dorian loved you. But if the roles were reversed and you disappeared, there's no way he would've done half of the things you have." Rosie's coughing fit wracked her fragile frame; her grip on Karma's hand weakened. Her next inhale rattled. "And think about the things you went through at Phoenix Corps. Would Dorian have survived that? I know the watered-down stories you've told me—and yes, I know you downplayed them to not scare me or the others. There's no chance he escaped from them either. Without you guiding him, he'd never find his way on his own."

"I don't even know if he's dead, Rosie. I could still be married."

"I should hope any man worth your time would have contacted you in *some* way by now. Before the quake, if your spouse disappeared, they could be declared dead after seven years with no communication. It's been over ten years now. You are free to move on." Rosie struggled to catch her breath, but refused to stop talking, waving away Karma's attempt to bring her water. "I knew you and Dorian before. You loved him. He loved you. But Dorian was *never* your partner, Karma. Ridge would be your partner."

"But Rosie..."

"No buts, Karma. Just think about what I've said. Now go. I'm going to rest my eyes for a bit in the quiet."

Tears filled Karma's eyes as she did what Rosie asked. Once back outside, she followed the scents of Ridge and the kids, finding them a couple of blocks away, tending to his impressive garden.

Lily and Peter ran to her, wrapping her in a hug, tears wetting their own faces, and the shoulders of her shirt. Her tears fell freely as she pulled the kids closer. The kids were resilient. They would get through this loss, just like they had any other. But when Rosie passed, and Karma knew it wouldn't be too long, she would leave a huge hole in their hearts.

Ridge appeared nearly as emotional as she did when he stepped up to them, as the kids stepped back. "Can you two gather some more sage?" he asked.

Peter and Lily headed back over to the beds, and Ridge stepped closer, his voice quiet. "Are you okay?"

Karma wiped angrily at her face, hating the weakness of the tears. "I knew she wasn't well. I didn't know it would be this soon. I mean, she's been showing symptoms for a couple of years, but still, it's too soon."

"Is she...?" he started.

"She asked me to go. To leave her to rest. Will she be there when we get back?" Karma looked over her shoulder, back the way she came, and shrugged. "I don't know." Karma leaned against the brick wall. "Before the quake, Mrs. Thorn was diagnosed with congestive heart failure. I helped as much as I could. I scavenged medications for her for a while.

"When Mrs. Thorn passed on, I'd only had Lily about a year, and Peter only a few weeks. Rosie helped so much, keeping the kids safe and occupied when I was away. When I started noticing the same symptoms in Rosie, I tried to get meds, but the meds I know to give either changed names or aren't available anymore."

"I want to help," he said, placing his hand lightly on her shoulder. "If you will let me."

The warmth and strength of his hand seeped into her body, making her want to step closer, to lean on him, letting him take some of her burdens, but she held herself rigid. "The kids really like you. You take care of them, are kind to them, and can keep them safe when I can't. I'd be stupid not to let you help."

His hand shifted, sliding to her neck, and he lifted his thumb under her chin, tipping it up until their eyes met. "While I really like the kids, they aren't the reason I'm here."

"I..." words failed her as she fell into the depths of his bright, green eyes. The vulnerability of his hand so close to her throat caused a shiver, but not the fear she expected.

"I get your hesitation. I won't push you. But I'm not going away either, Karma." He dropped his hand and turned back to the kids, calling for them to finish up as if his words, his touch, hadn't just rocked her to the core.

Rosie was gone.

Karma knelt next to the cot and took Rosie's cool hand in her own. "Thank you, dear friend. You were a light to us all. You will be missed." Karma pulled the blanket up over Rosie and trudged back to the stairs under the trap door, where Ridge stood.

He didn't speak. He simply gathered her in his arms, lending her his strength and warmth.

Karma wasn't sure she'd ever be warm again.

"The kids will want to say goodbye."

She took a step back and cleared the lump from her throat. "Send them down. I'll stay with them. Then I'll take her to rest near Mrs. Thorn.

Ridge's hand trailed lightly over her cheek, wiping away the residual tears and adding new ones with his gentleness. "I can take her."

Karma shook her head. "No. I will do it." Her eyes lifted to his blazing green ones. She swallowed hard at the mix of emotion swirling in their depths. Her voice barely above a whisper, Karma said, "Thank you for the offer. It means a lot."

"She was a special lady."

"That she was." Karma turned her back to him, refusing to allow herself to fall into his arms. He was strong enough to take the burden, to help her, but her responsibilities still stood in the way. "Send them down."

Lily and Peter clung to her, tears flooding their eyes as they each held Rosie's cooling hand and said their goodbyes.

Peter was the first to step away, and he went straight to Ridge, hiding his face in Ridge's chest.

Ridge rubbed Peter's back, comforting him, but his eyes never left Karma's.

She swallowed hard at the intensity of his gaze.

When Lily stepped away, she picked up the weaving Rosie had started and sat down on the nearby sofa, picking up where Rosie left off.

"I'll take her to Mrs. Thorn. You two stay with Ridge for now."

Karma gathered Rosie into her arms.

Thankfully, Ridge stayed where he was, only moving to open the door. He rested his hand on the small of her back, its warmth seeping through the fabric to her skin, steadying her as she climbed the steep stairs to the surface.

"I'll return as soon as I can. I need to check on Annabeth before I come back, though."

"Karma," Ridge waited until she turned to look at him before continuing. "Take whatever time you need. I'll keep the kids safe. You don't need to worry about hurrying back."

She dipped her head in acknowledgement, struggling to keep the tears at bay.

Rosie's words repeated in her head. "*Dorian was never your partner, Karma. Ridge would be your partner.*"

Chapter 26

5713

Karma

Karma made short work of digging a spot near Mrs. Thorn and placed Rosie's blanketed body inside, covering her with the earth robotically. But not before she found a piece of paper tucked into Rosie's hand. In her shaky handwriting, Rosie had left her with one final note.

He's a good one, Karma. Trustworthy. Find the light in this dreary world and hold onto it with both hands. You've done it all by yourself for too long.

She'd operated on autopilot since leaving the trap door, walking away from Ridge and the kids, but the note brought a new bout of tears.

Karma stopped in Mrs. Thorn's trailer to clean up before making her way to her own, where Annabeth was still very weak, even though her animal was so developed in her. The fevers were less severe but kept coming in the night with no sign of letting up yet. She'd barely slept the night before, watching over Annabeth and now with Rosie gone...

Knowing she would need to reenter Phoenix Corp soon for supplies was a welcome distraction from the sadness.

Karma gave Annabeth the soup she had heated and got her back into bed to rest. She moved to the bedroom on the far side of the trailer, the one without a bed and rarely used. Grabbing a darker colored, long-sleeved shirt from the closet, she pulled it on over her t-shirt and grabbed one of the bags she kept for when she went "shopping."

Ridge's scent hit her full on. He was here, somewhere. Karma moved to the side of the trailer, finding him in the garden, tending to the herbs.

"Peter and Lily are back at my place. They are safe," he said, as she walked into view.

"I'm going to get some supplies. I'll be back by morning. Annabeth is sleeping again. Hopefully, she'll stay that way. I'll drop supplies by your place too."

Ridge snagged her hand when she turned to leave. "It's too dangerous right now. They are looking for you. Especially since you've snuck in and out so many times recently."

"The kids need to eat. So do we. I'll be fine."

"Damnit, Karma! Listen to me."

"Tell me how I can feed everyone without going back in there? How can I get clothes to replace those we've had to cut up or burn?"

Ridge closed the distance between them, crowding her in when she stepped back, her back pressed against the trailer. "It's dangerous."

"It's always dangerous."

"You know what I mean." Frustration bled through his tone. He caged her in with his arms, his heat surrounding her.

For once, she stepped into his heat, Rosie's words echoing in her head. "I need you to keep the kids safe while I'm gone." She nearly drowned in the depths of his eyes when he tilted her chin with his rough fingers to meet their gazes.

"You know I will."

Karma rose to her tiptoes and reached up, pulling him to her, initiating their kiss this time. She buried

her hand in the short strands of his hair, the softness tickling her fingers, fisting the other in the soft
material of his shirt.

Ridge growled, plunging his tongue into her mouth,
his arms like steel bands pulling her to him, holding
her there. His hardness became evident against her
stomach as he pinned her to the trailer wall with his
hips. He pulled at her hair, deepening the angle and
their kiss.

Desperation gripped her.

Ridge's hand dropped to her waist, pulling her shirt
out of her waistband and connecting flesh on flesh.
His hand skimmed the skin of her lower back, sending sparks along her nerve endings all the way to her
toes. When it coasted along her side, up her ribs,
and grazed the side of her breast, she trembled.

She whimpered when his hand moved, losing contact with her skin, and gasped when his hands slid
over the backs of her thighs, lifting her off the
ground in one quick motion.

Never breaking the kiss, Ridge carried her to the
other trailer and shouldered his way in, kicking the
door shut behind him and throwing the lock lever.
He slid her down his body until her feet hit the floor,
both trembling at the sensations whirring through
them. Ridge sucked her bottom lip and nipped light-

ly at it, then pulled back and dropped his forehead to hers, their labored breathing in sync.

"You don't have to go now."

She caressed the side of his face. "You know I do. You know we need food and supplies."

"Let me go," he pleaded.

"Do you know a dozen different ways in and out of there without being seen?" Her question was spoken softly.

He closed his eyes and gave a nearly imperceptible shake of his head.

"If I know you are there to take care of the kids, I can do my job. I can get supplies."

He kissed her, long and languid. "Draw me a map of all the ways in and out. When you come out this time, take the time to teach me the map. You don't get to continue to take all the risks. You will let me help you. Agreed?"

"I can't ask you to put yourself at risk. You don't owe me anything."

"You aren't asking, Karma. And I've been hiding since I left Phoenix Corps. You've given me back a real life, people to care about. I care about the kids. I *care* about you. I'm asking *you* to let me help you."

The pleading in his eyes stole her breath. In him, she saw the light in her dreary world, just like Rosie said. She clasped his hands in hers and tugged him closer again, wrapping her arms around him. "Thank you," she whispered.

Ridge stepped back and lifted the door to the tunnel. He led the way, pulling her behind him.

In a blur of motion, he spun, pulling her into his arms as they crossed the threshold into the underground room. His lips crashed into hers while his hands burrowed back under her shirt, bringing with them the fireworks along her nerve endings.

Karma tugged at the hem of his soft shirt, needing to touch his skin.

Ridge stepped away, pulling his shirt over his head, followed by hers.

Her eyes caught on the powerful muscles of his arms and chest. She reached out, gliding her fingers over the translucent skin covering the site of the wounds left by Pip's bite. The muscles beneath her fingers bunched and twitched at the contact. Her fingers curled at the memory of him just the week before, pulse thready and fever spiking with infection. Her eyes burned at the memory of how close he'd come to dying.

Ridge let her look her fill but pulled her back against him when the first tears fell.

"We almost lost you, too."

He pressed kisses to her forehead, cheeks, and lips. "I'm here. I'm healthy. And you can't get rid of me that easily. I'm pretty persistent, if you hadn't caught on yet." His cocky smirk made her grin.

"I hadn't noticed."

His growl rumbled through his chest, lifting her and depositing her on the cot she usually slept on, lowering himself onto her and claiming her mouth again.

Their hands and mouths roamed, discovering each other, bringing sighs, tingles, and heat trailing behind.

While it had been a long time since Karma had been intimate with anyone, she never remembered the intensity she was feeling with Ridge. He was patient, learning how she reacted to each touch of his fingers, lips, and tongue as he removed the rest of their clothing.

She could almost hear his purr as she wrapped her calf around his thigh, pulling him tighter, seating him fully within her, drawing out her own sigh.

He moved in smooth motions, watching her face for every reaction, adjusting the angle and speed, heightening her pleasure. Ridge swallowed her cries of pleasure as she crested, his movements becoming erratic and swift until he followed her over, collapsing on her. He wrapped her tight against him, shifting his body so they lay side by side on the narrow cot, waiting for their breathing to slow.

In the darkness, he told her, "You can't run from me anymore. You can't push me away, Karma. I'm here to stay. You understand that, right?" His fingers trailed over her sweat-slick skin, raising goose bumps along his path.

"I've been alone a long time, Ridge. You may have to remind me from time to time," she replied into his chest.

His finger came to rest at her chin, tilting it up until their eyes met in the darkness, his glowing an eerie green. He lowered his mouth to hers in a lingering kiss that made her toes curl. "I'll remind you every moment of every day, if that's what it takes."

Chapter 27

Karma

Karma inched out of Ridge's arms, so as not to wake him. She couldn't even see his outline in the pitch darkness of the room. She claimed her clothes from the pile on the floor and made her way into Mrs. Thorn's trailer.

Once there, she hurriedly sketched a map of Phoenix Corps and a few ways she used to get in, leaving it on the counter for Ridge to find when he came up. Karma tucked her hair up into an old ball cap and, with her handy shopping bag, headed out into the night.

Still full dark and a cloudy night, she had no light to navigate by. Karma followed memory and her nose as she traipsed through the streets, making her way toward Phoenix Corps.

Karma breezed past the park and dashed into the alleyway across from it. She hopped over three old, rusted-out cars that were crammed into some sort of barrier she never understood and crossed over another two streets before altering her path again. This path would take her across the service road near where she and Ridge crossed when they'd left Phoenix Corps together, past the drainage tunnel she used to escape. She darted across the street and down the embankment, following it along the road until the drainage tunnel came into view.

Something was off. Karma crouched down and made her way closer to the tunnel's exit. Son of a bitch. Anger rose. The tunnel was bricked up except for two small openings in the base with rebar grates inside to allow water to flow out, but nothing was getting in.

She checked her surroundings, looking for anything else out of the ordinary.

Her mind spun. She'd just come through here. They never showed any suspicion that she used this as an exit.

The steel gate she'd carried Ridge through still hung just behind the brick wall, mocking her. Her temper seethed. Ridge. She'd brought *him* through here.

That bastard. She'd let him in. She'd trusted him. She'd left the kids in his care! She'd slept with him! He betrayed her. He'd told them how she'd gotten him out, and they blocked it. She tried to wrack her brain for when he would have had an opportunity to give them the information since she'd dragged him out of Phoenix Corps this way. He'd been laid up and sick, then he'd been with the kids and Rosie.

She growled in frustration. If he'd left the kids and Rosie alone to betray her...

The mortar wasn't fully cured near the top. This wall had been built within the last two days or so. Phoenix Corps would have erected the wall as soon as they knew it was a vulnerability, so that meant he'd had to sneak away recently, when Rosie was so sick, leaving the kids alone with her. Karma's blood boiled with rage.

Sure, she had other ways to get out, but she'd now left him a map with several of her other paths labeled. He could hand them that map now and severely limit her ways in and out. If he gave them the map while she was still inside now...

How stupid could she be? How could he have be-trayed her? An ache built in her chest. Even on her trek here, her body still hummed with the memory of Ridge and his touch. Now, she wanted a shower in the worst way.

Her heart pounded. Did she go back and get the kids? Continue on? They could survive a bit on the stuff they could catch, but not much beyond herbs grew well. She relied on the food she stole from Phoenix Corps to keep the kids healthy. Indecision paralyzed her until she heard a convoy of trucks coming up the supply road, from the barge dock, toward the guard gate. There were several trucks in a line, and it would take a while for them to all clear the gate.

Making sure to stay out of the lights casting off the trucks, Karma scurried up the other side of the embankment and kept low, army-crawling through the fields, into the next copse of trees. The trees were sparser than those near the park, but there was enough cover for her to stand and run, weaving until she hit the last of the tree line.

Karma checked both ways and believed her nose when it told her there hadn't been anyone around in a while.

She emerged into the open air, stepping over the remains of mangled train tracks and train cars haphazardly tossed during the shaking of the quake and never repaired or set right.

Karma didn't like this entrance; there were too many places someone could hide to ambush her, but she hadn't used it in a long time. There was no way Ridge would've known to tell anyone about it. She hadn't even added this one to the map she'd hastily scrawled for him yet.

Crawling under the first car she came to, Karma slithered her way to the other side and popped to her feet. The next three cars were tipped over onto their sides. She climbed up and over each of them. The last, she climbed through one of the broken windows and into the interior, which smelled worse every time she came this way. The broken glass allowed the rainwater to enter, soaking the once plush and opulent fabrics covering the fancy seats. The mold and mildew grew with each rainstorm. The brass inside was all oxidized, turning a putrid greenish-brown and no longer smooth to the touch. Karma climbed over and around the swampy seats, carefully avoiding touching anything as much as possible, and exited through the door, hanging from one lonely hinge.

Once her feet were back on the ground, she moved over the twisted tracks and around the other cars between her and her destination. Karma made her way up to the fencing on this side of the property and slid through a gap she'd created a few years before. The vines covering it from inside the property were enough to hide it, unless someone was specifically looking for a break in the fence.

The heat and motion sensors would be active at this time of night, so she made her movements as small as possible, crouching low and moving quickly to the shed she knew would not only hide her position but also give her the way in.

The people at Phoenix Corps were so arrogant that they never checked the locks, just assuming they were locked behind them. Karma took full advantage of that. She'd rigged it years ago so that the door wouldn't latch anymore, but it still looked locked and closed.

Karma pulled the door open easily and slipped inside. Large pipes stuck up out of the ground with large red valves attached. Severe cracks spider-webbed through the concrete slab of the floor, unable to withstand the shifting from the aftershocks. She wove through the pipes to the hunk of concrete she was looking for and wedged her fingers in the right spot.

Her anger fueled her strength almost as much as the altering had. The slab lifted easily. Solid-packed dirt lay under one side of the slab, but the other was a concrete-lined chase for the pipes to run through, down into an underground maintenance tube.

She climbed into the chute, locking her legs around one of the pipes so she could pull the slab back into place. Once fully seated and concealed, Karma released the pressure in her legs and slid down the pipe like an old firehouse pole, dropping to the floor below. The large, concrete-lined room fed into a maintenance tube about twenty feet away.

The maintenance tube was made of corrugated metal and was barely tall enough for her to stand in. Electrical and plumbing conduits ran the entire length, branching off into other, smaller tubes the closer she got to the building. She followed the main lines for what seemed like an eternity, questioning her decision not to go back for the kids every step of the way.

Ridge had every opportunity to take the kids to Phoenix Corps for the last few days, and he hadn't. They should be safe for a bit. He also didn't know that Karma was aware of his betrayal. He had no reason to try to use the kids as leverage against her, and by the time he found out she knew, she'd have the kids back under her care, and he'd be dying a slow and painful death at her hands. Not only had he made it infinitely more difficult for her to get into or out of the Phoenix Corps compound, but she'd have to abandon the trailer park and find a new place to hole up and keep the kids safe. All the work she'd put in to build the tunnel under the trailer, to build a safe, secure home for Lily and Peter...

She clenched her hands, gritting her teeth, and tried to clear any thoughts of him from her mind. Karma couldn't afford any distractions while she was inside enemy territory. She needed to focus on the task at hand.

Just before the conduits dropped into the main maintenance room on this level, she veered off, following a smaller branch of the pipes. The main room housed the water pipes, whereas a room down the way held the electrical panel. That was her destination. To the left of where the conduits punched through the wall, a small access hatch door allowed her into the room filled with noisy servers and fans on rows and rows of black steel racks.

Karma carefully climbed the rack on the end and popped out one of the drop ceiling tiles. A rat's nest of wires crisscrossed this area, so she moved slowly, careful not to pull any of the wires from their connections to the servers below. Once she was secure in her perch inside the ceiling, Karma replaced the ceiling tile. If she were careful, no one would be the wiser that anyone came through here.

She made her way from beam to beam of the steel framework within the ceiling, dodging more pipes and wires along the way. Stealth was required. She heard the voices of people in the rooms below as she picked her way along.

Reaching the maintenance ladder, she climbed up floor by floor until she reached the level of the loading dock, but she was clear on the other side of the building. Karma weaved her way over, under, and through several beams before lifting a tile and dropping into the room below. This storage room contained the clothes she would need.

She grabbed new shoes for herself, a few tops that would work for her or Lily, and some things for Peter. She reached for a shirt that would fit Ridge, to replace the one she'd had to cut off after the fight with Pip. She curled her fingers against her palm and squeezed. Her belly fluttered with the memory of his skin against her palm, his lips against hers.

Karma shook the memory off. He betrayed her. She'd never forgive that. She fought the urge to topple the shelves in anger. Instead, she grabbed some clothes for Peter and stuffed them into the bag as well, and made her way back into the ceiling.

Food was next on her shopping list. Then she'd have to get back into the ceiling and work her way over to one of the other exits, unable to use the drainage tunnel.

Bastard! He'd done so much damage by divulging her secrets. It was the easiest way out of the building. A way Phoenix Corps still hadn't discovered and how she escaped them the first time—how she continued to escape time and again.

Tucking the bag tight to her body so it wouldn't hit anything and make noise, Karma reentered the ceiling and began the arduous maze leading to one of the storage rooms she liked to 'shop' from. Passing the maintenance ladder she'd used the last time she was here, she paused, something catching her attention at the corner of her eye.

Karma froze in place and turned her head. Fuck.

Chapter 28

Karma

A camera. They'd placed cameras in the ceiling.

Heads popped up into the ceiling, like a creepy game of whack-a-mole, her foot and fist connecting with as many as she could reach. She made it to the top of a wall and skittered backwards, balancing on the narrow board at the top.

The sickly smell of body odor and saltwater reached her just as Pip broke through a ceiling tile behind her, grabbed her by the neck, and dragged her down into the office below.

"Well, pet, it seems like you just can't keep away from here. You miss us that much, *pet*?" Pip's foul breath wafted in front of her face, the vile smell urging her to lose what little she'd eaten.

Karma stomped on Pip's feet, wrenching her body to dislodge his hold on her.

Pip held fast, and moments later, the goon squad joined him, further pinning her limbs and limiting her movement. The sharp jab of a needle into her neck brought a sensation of falling, and then nothing.

Voices were the first things to penetrate the darkness she drowned in. Karma stifled a groan at the pain radiating in her skull and the stiffness in the arms and legs she couldn't move. The strap tightly binding her chest hindered her ability to take a deep breath. The same type of strap dug painfully into her hips and pelvis. A gag tore at the corners of her lips.

Karma blinked open her eyes, the bright light momentarily blinding her. Two people wearing lab coats that she didn't recognize stood on one side of the room, talking over a clipboard'. Like most of the lab people, they were fully human, unaltered. And she could smell Pip. He wasn't in the room, but he hadn't been gone for long.

She tugged experimentally at her arms, but she couldn't twist them at all. The leather restraints had been replaced with steel manacles.

Karma tried folding her hands, making them narrower, so she could pull them out of the manacles, to no avail.

"I wouldn't try that if I were you," one of the lab techs said, walking past and whacking her with the clipboard on her nose, like she was a dog.

When she got out of here, Pip was going to die.

Speaking of—in sauntered a smug Pip. His strange, too wide mouth showed his grotesque teeth. "So glad you're awake, pet. I want to make sure you are awake to enjoy this. I know I will." Pip ran his finger down her cheek, her neck, and then her arm. The oily feeling left behind made her desperate for a shower. Cranking on a lever, the manacles at her wrists tightened down more painfully than before.

Karma bit down on her bottom lip to keep from crying out at the pain. She breathed heavily, unwilling to give him the satisfaction of making noise.

Pip cranked the lever again.

Then she felt it—there was some kind of wedge or blade *inside* the manacles. The second crank had pushed whatever it was through the osteoderms under her human skin. Blood ran down the incline, pooling in her palm.

Pip crossed to the other side of the table and cranked down on that lever twice.

Karma saw stars in her vision.

A backhand stung her cheek. "Ah, ah, pet. You will be awake the whole time, or we'll just have to start over."

She glared at Pip, working her jaw, trying to get her teeth to cut through the gag. Karma didn't have serrated teeth like Pip, but she'd get through the damn thing, even if it killed her. Closing her eyes for a moment, she recentered herself as she had countless times in his "care."

The second backhand wasn't a surprise. He never did like that she could compartmentalize her pain. Pip liked to hear the screams, the whimpers, the cries. She didn't flinch. She didn't vocalize her pain in any way. Karma simply turned her face back to center and focused on a spot on the wall in front of her, allowing her mind to drift. She'd gotten good at this the last time she was trapped here, and to add a cherry on top, it drove Pip insane.

Time passed, but she had no idea how long. The clattering of an overturned tray of surgical tools flying across the room and crashing into the wall brought her back to the present. She cursed the gag in her mouth, preventing her from smiling at the frustration rolling off Pip as he stormed out of the lab and into the hallway beyond.

The two lab techs remained in the room, bandaging the worst of the injuries not covered by the manacles. They loosened the manacles enough to pull the blades from her skin, but no further. Neither spoke to her. The smaller of the two turned off the lights in the room, and both left her alone. If this followed the same pattern as before, she'd be left there for hours.

Karma tested the restraints again, but nothing had any give to it. She was stuck here until someone released her.

Her mind wandered as she waited alone in the dark. *Why were there cameras in the ceiling?*

Ridge hadn't been in the ceiling at any time with her. She didn't tell him about being in the ceiling. Annabeth had been with her in the ceiling, through the same tunnel she'd used for Ridge. But had she really been unaware? And that faint, familiar smell she'd caught outside, near the laundromat, belonged to Annabeth; she was sure of it now.

She closed her eyes and took as deep a breath as she could manage with the tight strap over her chest. Karma sifted through the smells in her memory from near the laundromat; there had been a familiar smell muted among the rest in that area. She'd dismissed it at the time, but now, she ground her teeth harder against the gag.

Flashes of memories came to her—Annabeth coming down the hall from the bathroom. Had her posture sagged further once she realized Karma was there, watching her? The fevers lessened, but her weakness remained. Or did it?

Annabeth was awfully strong when she was thrashing in the nightmare, when her fangs emerged. It didn't correlate to the weakness she showed any other time Karma was around.

Ridge didn't betray her. The kids would be safe with him. She could concentrate on getting herself out of this mess.

Chapter 29

7619

Ridge

She was gone.

Ridge knew before he opened his eyes. He lit one of the lanterns and found his clothes neatly folded in a pile. He dressed, then made his way up to Mrs. Thorn's kitchen. The piece of paper on the counter caught his attention. He smiled as he lifted it.

It was a crude map, but it was the map he'd asked for. And in the corner of it, she'd left him a note:

I'll draw you a better map when I get back. Thank you for everything you've done for us. Thank you for keeping the kids safe. I'm really grateful that you came into our lives... that you came into my life. I'll be back soon with supplies for us all.

Ridge tucked the map into the pocket of his worn jeans and slipped out into the cool night air. Dawn would be approaching soon, and he needed to get back to the kids, so he bypassed Karma's trailer and left the trailer park.

Lily was just stirring when Ridge dropped down the trap door. Peter was still softly snoring.

"You guys sleep okay? No incidents while I was gone?"

Lily shook her head. "Peter had a nightmare, but otherwise nothing out of the ordinary."

"Go ahead and heat a can of soup for you and Peter for breakfast. I'll check the traps later and hope we find some fresh meat in those to have something else for a change."

"You are starting to run low on cans. I know we have less than this at the trailer park, too."

"Yeah, we've noticed. Karma went shopping last night. She should be back soon with some extra supplies for us."

"She went back in already?" Lily's eyes were wide with fear.

"Not much choice with food running so low. But I'm going to make sure she's not the only one going in the future. Okay? I'm sticking around and helping out from now on."

"But last time..."

Ridge ducked his head a bit so he was eye to eye with Lily. "You know Karma. She's as badass as it gets." He chucked her under the chin. "I think the only reason Phoenix Corps is still standing is because it's her favorite store to shop at. Otherwise, she'd have blown it up long before now."

Lily smiled, the reaction he was aiming for. "You might be right about that. If not for the deliveries coming through to Phoenix Corps, we'd likely starve."

"Exactly. She'll be fine." He hoped he wasn't lying, but he couldn't ignore the uneasiness in his gut.

Lily and Peter were busy playing cards again when he headed to the surface to check on Annabeth and see if Karma had made it back yet. He figured she would go to his place first, to see the kids and drop off some supplies, but he hadn't heard anything yet.

Ridge made his way to the trailer park in the most direct, but still roundabout way he could manage. He was impatient to see if Karma was back. The path he took dropped him off on the other side of the park, and he approached Karma's trailer from a different angle. Not far from the bathroom window, he caught a scent that shouldn't be out there.

Ridge rounded the trailer and barged through the door to silence. Annabeth, absent from the bed, wasn't down the hall or in the now-empty bathroom. The secret panel in the hallway hadn't been disturbed, so she couldn't have gone out that way, but he already knew the answer.

The scent he caught was a mix of new and old smells, of the same smells. Annabeth had left out the bathroom window, and this wasn't the first time.

He ground his teeth together in irritation, clenching his fist, wanting to hit something. Instead, he turned on his heel and went back into the trailer, checking Mrs. Thorn's trailer and the tunnel, knowing she wouldn't be there, but hoping Karma was back and he just hadn't seen her yet.

His outrage grew when he entered the subterranean room where he'd spent a good bit of the night with Karma. Their scent mingled in the air, and he could still smell her on his skin. He slammed his fist into the wall of dirt, causing dirt to trickle down from the ceiling. He pulled his fist back and spun on his heel, getting outside in a flash. He hurried but carefully watched his surroundings as he made his way back to his place.

Passing by the laundromat, he caught the masked scents again, and they were mingled with another smell he'd missed before—Annabeth's.

Ridge fought back the panic and let the anger take hold. He'd need every ounce of rage he could muster. Someone would pay for this. A lot of someones. And he relished the thought of getting his hands directly on Pip or Annabeth. He'd just found Karma. He wasn't about to let her go now. He didn't know the first thing about taking care of Peter and Lily in the long run. He *needed* her.

Ridge dropped unceremoniously through the trap door, skipping the stairs entirely, startling Peter and Lily. He pulled the crudely drawn map from his pocket and spread it out on the table in front of Lily. "Is the route you left Phoenix Corps on this map?"

Lily's wide, scared eyes stared at him, her mouth gaping open and her hand white knuckled as she held on to Peter's arm.

Ridge softened his voice, pointing again at the map. "I need you to look at this map and tell me if the way you took to get out, the way Karma took to get in to find you, is drawn on here."

Lily's eyes dropped to the map, and a finger on the hand not grasping onto Peter shook as it moved to the side of the map, which had no markings yet.

"Karma?" Peter said, tears welling in his eyes.

"If she's in there, buddy, I'll bring her home. You have my word, okay?" He turned to Lily. "Point out as much to me as you can remember."

Lily's face was ghostly pale.

"Lily, I need you to show me what you know, okay? And then, I need you to keep Peter safe. You have enough cans for a few more days if you limit how much you eat a day. You do not leave this place under any circumstances. Am I clear?"

She nodded stiffly.

"Show me."

Ridge listened intently as Lily told him about the way she used to escape from Phoenix Corps facilities. He made notes on the edge of the page.

He stood to leave, but Lily's hand came down on the map, holding it in place. She tapped her finger on the words Karma had written to him. "She wouldn't say that to just anyone." Pointing to where Karma said she was grateful he was in *her* life.

"I know. I won't let her or you down. I'm bringing her back. Stay in here. Stay safe. We'll be back as soon as I can get her out of there."

Chapter 30

5713

Karma

Pip's stench hit her like a wall as the door closed behind him. Flipping on the light switch forced Karma to squint her eyes.

"Did you miss me, pet?" He leered at her, then tapped his forehead with a finger. "I can feel your heart rate increasing with each step I take." He took a step closer, and another.

Karma spat out the gag. "The foul odor coming off of you in waves is nauseating. I'm trying not to lose my lunch." Her nonchalant tone had its intended effect, irritating him. The backhand she received over her already bruised face was a consequence she was willing to take.

"We didn't give you lunch."

"And that is how nauseating you are. You make me want to lose my lunch from *days* ago."

Pip grabbed her chin, holding her face in a painful grip, and pressed his lips to her ear. "Wanna know how we finally caught you, pet? How we caught the others?" He smiled as he pulled back, likely picking up on the panic racing through her at the thought that Pip got his hands on Lily, Peter, and Ridge.

She clamped down on her emotions.

"We brought your kitty cat here, too. He's just a few doors down. You may even get to hear him scream."

Karma squeezed her eyes shut against the terror overwhelming her. If they had Ridge there wasn't anyone left to take care of the kids. They'd be on their own.

Her stomach roiled again.

Karma slammed her forehead into Pip's nose, smiling at the satisfying crack as it broke.

He reared back, grabbing towels to stem the blood freely flowing down his face. Holding the towel with one hand, he cranked the levers on her wrist manacles, driving the blades in deeper than before.

Karma ground her teeth against the pain but refused to utter a sound.

The click of the door caused her to look up, into eyes she recognized with oddly shaped pupils.

"Morning, Annabeth. Feeling better, I see." The casualness of her tone made Pip grind his teeth, and Karma smiled.

"I feel *much* better, no thanks to you," she replied. "If you had left my dad alone, he could have finished his treatment. He would have come home to me and never would have hurt me. You took him from me!"

"He would have killed you, Annabeth. He wasn't the same man you knew after Phoenix Corps got hold of him. And Annabeth, if they had finished altering him, he'd have never been returned to you."

"You killed him, you bitch! I swore from that moment on that I would make you suffer." Annabeth stepped forward and slapped her.

Karma's face was half numb from the prior blows Pip delivered. She barely noticed the swat from Annabeth, which only enraged her more.

An evil sneer pasted itself on Annabeth's face, and her fist connected with Karma's solar plexus. Her taunting whisper brushed over Karma's cheek. "I've been working for them for weeks. They brought me meds in exchange for information. They are making me stronger. What luck that I ran into Lily on my way to meet up with Brandy for my latest dose that night!

"As you 'rescued' me, you showed me every step you used to get out of here undetected. And that information earned me the best reward." Satisfaction rolled off Annabeth in waves. Her gloating made Karma nauseous. "It's only a matter of time until I take my turn with your boyfriend and the kids, too. We'll be sure to make you watch before we get rid of you for good."

Karma struggled to get loose from the bindings holding her in place as Annabeth laughed. Anger and panic warred for top billing in her emotions.

Annabeth stepped back and lifted the sleeve of her shirt, revealing a fresh tattoo, in iridescent ink on her forearm. The swirl of the snake across the P, C confirmed her suspicions that Annabeth, in more ways than one, was a snake.

Pip's sneer made her want to lash out, fight back, but her bindings left her with no recourse.

"We shared our food with you."

It was Annabeth's turn to sneer. "Food you stole from Phoenix Corps."

"Food that last I heard was supposed to be given freely to the people here in need. The people who are struggling to survive in this desolate wasteland."

"Oh, pet. You are so naive. The government doesn't give a shit about any of you. They only want the enhanced soldiers we are providing them with. They endorse what we're doing. Hell, they are helping to fund us. Andrew Phoenix might as well be the president. We're so much bigger than you even know." Pip cocked his head to the side. "Where's the other girl you took out of here? What did you do with her?"

Karma's stomach fluttered in relief. He didn't know about Lily. Neither did Annabeth. She hadn't seen Lily since Karma pulled her out. "She died. Your barbaric methods killed her."

Pip looked thoughtful for a moment. "If that's true, we should study her body. Where can we find it? We can set her up right here, right next to you, and perform the autopsy."

"I don't know how you find anything with your head so far up Phoenix Corps' ass."

This backhand was harder than the rest. The audible crack was more than from Pip's hand striking her. Karma's orbital bone cracked, and her eye immediately started to swell.

"You'd do well to watch your mouth, pet."

"I'm going to take great pleasure in killing you, Pip."

"You'll never get that chance."

The lab techs from the day before entered the room. Each one took a side and jabbed her in the arms with long needles, pushing and grinding them to get through the osteoderms and into the veins below. She couldn't stifle the quick intake of breath and the involuntary twitch the grinding caused.

Nausea rode her hard as they pushed some unknown concoction into the veins on both sides of her arms. The burning raced up her arms, across her chest, and up her neck.

A disembodied, agonizing scream penetrated the air, making her wish she could cover her ears, only to discover the sound came from her.

The maniacal laugh came from Pip, standing in front of her with a smug grin on his grotesque mouth. "Monitor her vitals. Another couple of doses and we'll see if there's been any change in her."

Sweat dripped from her, and only the bindings holding her in place kept her from curling into a fetal position and shaking.

"Pet, you are going to wish you fled the area when you had a chance. Remember how much it hurt—the days and weeks of injections, changing your DNA?" Pip lowered his voice and whispered in her ear, spiking her fear, then laughed and stepped back, shrugging. "This will probably kill you. But we'll have fun using you to perfect the procedure for your kitty cat friend."

Her body was wracked with pain; she couldn't open her mouth or lift her head to spit at the foul tyrant standing in front of her, and he knew it.

Pip laughed as he escorted Annabeth and the two technicians out of the lab, leaving her alone and shrouded in darkness again.

Only then did she let the tears fall.

Chapter 31

7619

Ridge

Climbing through the sewage system, Ridge was impressed with the detail Lily had provided him with. He was able to navigate the smelly, confined space to the mechanical room. He shed his clothes, changing into the clothes he'd brought wrapped in plastic to keep them clean and smell-free, and then pushed the boxes to cover his entrance.

The blue plate next to the door gave him his location within the building. He was intimately familiar with Lower Level Three.

He listened at the door. The echoes of footsteps ended with a closed door down the hall, leaving only silence behind. Ridge cracked the door open to be sure, then pushed out and headed away from the labs. Lily told him she was kept one level lower. If he knew Pip and the rest, they'd be putting Karma in the room that would do the most harm mentally—the room they'd kept Lily in.

Ridge skirted his way down the hall, avoiding the cameras where possible and obscuring his face when he couldn't. He entered one of the many stairwells and worked his way down one level to where Lily explained she'd been kept.

The hallway on this level was busier, and he had to wait almost ten minutes before the coast was clear. But when he finally broke the seal, pushing the door open, he was hit full on with Pip's scent and the metallic tang of terror. Hidden among the pungent smell of Pip was the faint scent of Annabeth. But the terror was Karma.

Rage boiled Ridge's blood. Red tinged his vision. He took a deep breath to rein in his anger and inched the door open bit by bit. He followed his nose, tracking Pip back the way he came.

Peering in the window of the door he stopped at, it was dark inside, but there she was, strapped down to a table. Dark tracks trailed from the inside of her elbow to the manacles clamping her hands in place, a dark spot marred the palm of each hand, and her head hung down.

Ridge didn't need to summon his outrage to aid his strength. He pushed down on the handle, smiling at the satisfying crack when the handle broke off in his hand. Crossing the distance without turning on the light, Ridge tucked his finger under Karma's chin, lifting her face. A great purplish bruise and swelling darkened the left side of her face. Blood dripped from the corners of her mouth, and tears tracked down her face. When his hand fell away from her chin, her head dropped back down, a barely audible whimper escaping her cracked and dry lips.

"I'm here," he said softly, "I'm getting you out of here, baby." Ridge tipped the table back until it was almost horizontal.

He tore the straps securing her to the table.

Karma rewarded him by taking a deep breath.

He touched the lesser bruised cheek on the right, gently brushing away the fresh tracks of tears. Setting back to the task at hand, Ridge tried to pry at the manacles securing her wrists.

Karma's quick intake of breath caused him to examine the shackle further. He unsheathed the sharp claws from beneath his fingernails and sliced at the fabric lining the inside of the metal band. The metal blade embedded in her wrist gleamed with her blood even in the limited light in the room. Cursing, he found the lever used to tighten the blade and quickly loosened it.

Fresh blood flowed around the cuff.

Ridge pried the shackle open and quickly bandaged her wrist to stem the flow of blood. He repeated the process with the other side. He caught her as her whole body drooped lifelessly, keeping her from sliding further down the table, which was only at a slight incline. He pushed the table fully flat and moved to her feet, prying each of her legs free.

He pressed a light kiss to her forehead and wrapped his arms around her, lifting her to a seated position. "Karma, baby, I need you to give me the quickest way out of here."

She whimpered and gave the slightest shake of her head.

Holding her upright with one hand, he used the other to lift her chin. "Karma, look at me." Ridge pressed, command in his tone.

"It's gone. Take care of them. Leave me."

"Not a chance in hell, baby. You are leaving with me. I need you to be my map."

Ridge pulled her off the table, but her legs wouldn't hold her weight, and she slumped to the ground. He bent, pulling one of her arms over his shoulders and wrapping his arm around her waist.

Karma slumped forward and dry heaved.

When she finished, he lifted her head to look in her eyes, checking her pupils for signs of concussion. She flinched away when he turned the light on to look.

"No concussion."

"They injected me with something. It burned."

Ridge couldn't help the rumble in his chest. "Who?"

"Pip. Who else?" The incredulity in her tone penetrated, despite the exhaustion and weakness of her body.

"I'll kill him."

"Get in line." The anger in her voice made him smile.

"That's my girl."

"Annabeth..."

"I know. She'll get hers, too."

Ridge pulled her arm back over his shoulders and, wrapping his arm around her waist, took her weight and shouldered his way back out into the hall-way. With their height difference, he was forced to crouch. He debated just carrying her, but he needed at least one arm free for whatever they might encounter.

Her voice was quiet when she asked, "How did you get free?" Confusion must have been written across his face, because she continued, "Pip said you were in another room."

"He lied. I've been with the others. Keeping them safe, like you asked." He tightened his hold on her and kept walking to the stairs he used.

"I thought he had you." Her voice broke.

Ridge pulled her with him into the stairwell and leaned into her, against the wall. "I told you, you aren't getting rid of me. I'm here to stay and persistent as hell."

The weak smile she gave squeezed his heart. "I'm glad."

He bent to kiss her, but alarms blared, and lights flickered.

"Go up."

Ridge hurried up the stairs. Karma tried to take some of her own weight, but she was just too weak to sustain it or move quickly.

The hallway leading to the maintenance room he'd entered through was crowded with hordes of goon squad members.

"They know I got someone out that way, but they don't know how yet."

"I can't take them all on my own."

"Keep moving up."

Ridge took the stairs two at a time. Goon squad idiots lined the halls around the stairwell for the next two floors as well.

On the third floor up, the ground level, Karma urged him to stop. "There are more places to exit on this floor, if we can get to them. They've blocked off the way I got you out. But there are windows in some of the offices."

"I've got a better idea." Ridge checked through the narrow window on the door, peering as far as he could down the hallway. "There are three out there. Biff, Brandy, and someone else I don't know."

"Leave me here..."

"No!" he interrupted fiercely.

"You can't fight while holding me up." Karma placed her hand on the side of his face, the most she'd moved since he'd freed her from the torture table.

"Obviously, come back for me. But leave me here until you clear the hallway."

Ridge placed a gentle kiss on her abused lips. "Stay out of trouble."

"Not likely."

He propped her up against the wall next to the door, thankful her legs held her upright with the wall to lean on, and burst through the door. Ridge shoved the unknown guy into Brandy, sending them both sprawling across the floor, and grabbed Biff by the scruff of his neck, slamming his head through the emergency glass covering the fire extinguisher and hose.

Brandy, back on her feet, drove a shoulder into Ridge's kidneys.

Ridge grabbed the hose nozzle, yanking it free, and spun. He looped the hose, pulling it tight like a noose around first Brandy's hand, then her leg. Using her momentum against her, he spun Brandy and captured the other leg and hand in a similar knot, effectively hog-tying her.

Biff dove at him, blood pouring down his face from a nasty gash over his eyebrow, driving Ridge into the wall with a thud, hard enough to steal his breath.

Ridge spiked his elbows down into Biff's shoulder blade, drawing out an "Oompf." He stuck out his foot, tripping the other goon, knocking Biff off balance. Ridge grabbed the fire extinguisher and slammed it into the back of Biff's head, bouncing Biff's forehead off the floor.

The unknown goon's fist connected with Ridge's cheek. Pain exploded behind his eye. He swung his elbow around, connecting with the guy's jaw, hearing a satisfying crack of bone. Ridge jammed the fire extinguisher into his gut, but the guy latched onto it, refusing to release it.

Grabbing up near the nozzle, Ridge sheared the top off, causing thick powder to explode from the unit, giving the air a metallic taste. He'd closed his eyes, but the goon hadn't. Screams erupted, and Ridge kicked out, his foot connecting with the metal cylinder, jamming it further into the goon's gut.

Ridge spun, moving into the stairwell and grabbing Karma. "Hold your breath and close your eyes."

"What is all over you?" She dusted the powder covering his shoulder.

"Just listen for once, please."

Chapter 32

Karma

She held on to Ridge, her face tucked against his powder-covered shirt, as he burst through the door into the next section of the hallway, the door slamming behind them.

Ridge set her on her feet, leaning her against the silver metal shelves. The odor of Pip invading her nose clued her in to the reason Ridge stiffened before setting her on her feet.

He stalked forward, eyes locked on Pip, rage dripping from him, permeating the air.

Pip threw the first punch, connecting with Ridge's jaw. Ridge had time to move, but he didn't. He took the punch square on the jaw and answered with a hard fist to Pip's gut, doubling him over. Ridge's elbow connected with Pip's bottom jaw, snapping his head back.

The two men exchanged punches, elbows, and kicks, while Karma watched in horror.

Pip's teeth clamped down on Ridge's forearm. Ridge turned, driving Pip's head into the block wall. Pip's foot connected with the outside of Ridge's knee, taking him down, then pulled a leather strap from his lab coat pocket and wrapped it around Ridge's neck, tightening it.

Ridge scraped at the leather strap with his claws, leaving angry cuts on his neck, his face turning red, his eyes bulging. Ridge threw his weight, crashing into the walls, the floor, trying to buck Pip off.

In the chaos, Karma pulled apart a section of the shelving she was propped up on, grasping desperately onto the piece of piping she pulled free. She stumbled forward, unnoticed by Pip.

When he was within reach, Karma shoved the end of the pipe into Pip's eye socket with a sickening squish.

He screamed, grabbing at the offending pipe.

Ridge turned and kicked out at Pip's back, driving him face-first into the wall. Silence echoed through the hall.

A thick red line, visible through the fine white powder still covering Ridge, covered the circumference of his neck with vicious welts crisscrossing it. Karma reached out and touched it gently.

"You rescued me yet again," he said. "I'm good. Let's get out of here." He tucked his arm back around her and moved them through a couple more, luckily deserted, hallways.

They stood outside Pip's office. One more set of doors.

The sound of the screeching dock doors and diesel engines invaded the quiet hallway they stood in.

"Get me out there," Karma said, pointing at the door in front of them.

Ridge burst through the doors, startling a few dock workers.

Karma pushed away from Ridge and pointed at the box truck just backing up to the dock. "Get the driver out. We're leaving in that!"

She stumbled forward and fell more than jumped off the empty bay next to it.

Someone lowered the bay exit door; the reverse direction sounded worse than when it went up.

Karma ripped at a tire iron, pulling it from its mounting on the wall, and swung it in a wide arc. The wounds in her wrists throbbed in time with her heart, and the small amount of adrenaline pushing her began to wane.

The dock workers around her backed off, giving her a wide berth.

She made her way to the last bay, two bays from the truck, and with as much strength as she could muster, Karma slammed the tire iron against the valve of the propane tank anchored into the wall. The valve bounced off the wall and clattered onto the ground, gas spewing into the loading dock, now sealed shut by all the doors.

The remaining workers scattered as Karma stumbled her way back to the truck.

Ridge bent from the driver's seat, wrapping his arm around her, hauling her up and over his lap.

"Drive! Scrape the steel of the back bumper against the steel of the door track!" She shouted over the roar of the engine he'd kept running.

The engine gunned, and metal screeched, the aluminum front bumper colliding with the aluminum bay door.

Sparks flew as the back end of the box truck cleared the bay door frame, scraping the track. The concussion of the explosion lifted the back end of the vehicle clear off the ground, skidding the front tires forward and propelling the truck even faster.

"You sure know how to make an exit, baby," Ridge said, taking her hand and squeezing it.

The adrenaline keeping Karma going ran out about five seconds after Ridge drove through the guard station, scattering guards, leaving shards of wood and metal in their wake. The exhaustion overwhelming her stole the volume from her voice. "What are the chances this truck is full of food?"

"We'll find out soon. Just rest for a bit. You're safe now."

She felt safe with him, and blessed darkness took over her consciousness.

Chapter 33

7619

Ridge

Driving around the maze of rubble and broken-down cars in the streets took too long, in his opinion. Ridge wanted to get Karma back to his place, to safety, where she could rest. He kept peeking over at Karma. She seemed to be in a healing sleep, folded up in the passenger seat, strapped in, so she couldn't fall out of the seat while he drove.

Ridge parked the big truck a couple of blocks from his place. He didn't think anyone would be coming after them right away, but he didn't want to take the chance.

She barely stirred when he pulled her out of the truck to carry her, though she snuggled into his arms, bringing a smile to his face. He'd tried not to think about what had been done to her while she was in the hands of Pip and Phoenix Corps. But now, his hands shook with the possibilities of what *could have* happened to her if he hadn't gotten to her in time.

He crouched down, holding her tight to him, and opened the trap door. Descending the stairs, he noticed Lily, in fighting stance, standing between any potential threat and Peter. He smiled at her, and relief washed over her face.

Peter and Lily swarmed them, rapid-firing questions after questions.

Ridge readjusted Karma's weight and held up a hand to stall the questions. "I think Karma will be fine. But she didn't have an easy time in there, so I'll need help keeping an eye on her."

They nodded in unison.

He carried her over to the cot he used and laid her down, tucking blankets around her, gliding his hand over her silky hair. He stood back and turned to the kids. "I've got to go back to the truck we took and see what's in it. I need you guys to stay down here with Karma and keep an eye on her for me, would you?"

Upon returning to the truck, Ridge was pleased to find boxes of food and clothing. He took several trips, taking as much as he could fit into his hidey hole and hiding the rest in various other locations he'd used before. After stripping the truck of everything they might be able to use, he drove it back down near the service road and abandoned it, taking a roundabout way back to Karma and the kids. He stopped at the trailer park, where he boxed up what was left and hauled them back to his place. He stopped by the other occupied trailers, advising them to find a new place to hole up. He wasn't sure if any of them would believe him, after all, he'd never met them, but he hoped they would listen. For their sakes.

The kids sat vigil over Karma the entire time he was gone.

He approached them after setting down the box from the trailer.

"Why is she still sleeping?" Lily asked, her worry bleeding into her voice. "What happened to her face?"

"She didn't have an easy time in there. She's sleeping to give her body time to heal."

"Will she be okay?" Peter asked. His voice was more childlike than Ridge remembered hearing before.

"She's the toughest person I know. If anyone can heal these injuries, it's her."

Peter tucked himself against Ridge's side, and Ridge ruffled his hair.

"Should I make something to eat?" Lily asked.

"There's lots of food now, so yeah. Why don't you and Peter get some stuff heated up for us, and I can keep an eye on Karma for you?"

Lily held out her hand to Peter. "Come on and help me search the boxes and see what will make the tastiest dinner." False excitement rang in her voice, but it worked, and Peter joined her.

That left Ridge. He sat next to her, cradling her small hand in his. Turning her hand over, he unwound the hastily applied bandage, cleaned, and redressed the wounds with the supplies from the first aid kit he found in the truck. Ridge did his best to ignore the worry eating away at him. The kids didn't need to see it. They worried enough. He could see it in the way they'd both stop and watch Karma in the middle of doing another task, in the furrow of Lily's brow, and the fidgeting of Peter's hands. He'd gotten to know these kids, and they'd wormed their way into his heart, just like Karma had.

A small whimper caught his attention, and he turned back to her.

He knelt next to the cot, barely touching her hair with his hand, afraid to hurt her. "Shh, you're safe."

"Annabeth. The kids can't go back to the trailer." The sound coming from her was hoarse and weak.

"I brought anything you might need from the trailer. It's all here now. You are staying here with me. You all are."

"I'm sorry," she whispered.

"I wouldn't have it any other way."

Her head subtly shook back and forth. "I'm sorry," she repeated. "I doubted you. I saw the tunnel was bricked up. I thought you betrayed me, told them how I got out. It wasn't until after I found the cameras in the ceiling that I knew it couldn't have been you. It was Annabeth. I'm so sorry."

"You've been through the wringer in the last decade. Your trust is hard-earned."

Karma reached out with her hand, resting it on his. "You've earned it. Thank you." She rewarded him with a soft, shy smile.

Ridge heard the exhaustion in her further softening voice. He placed a soft kiss on her forehead and gently closed the one eye that would open. "Sleep now. I'll keep everyone safe."

"I know you will."

The quiet words made him feel like a superhero.

Chapter 34

5713

Karma

Itching. Itching all over. She could feel her heartbeat in her face, her wrists. Her mouth felt like the desert. But the itching...

She reached up to scratch at a spot on her neck and felt dry mud crumble away.

A hand lay over her arm, not grasping, just holding it. She felt weak as a baby, unable to pull her arm away from even the lightest touch.

Karma tried not to groan at the pain radiating down her body as she turned her head to see who touched her. The eye on that side of her head wouldn't open.

Ridge.

"You're safe. The kids are safe. You've had high fevers for days. You are going to be weak," he explained.

Her head too heavy to lift, Karma closed her eyes, fighting off tears. "I haven't been this weak since before I went to Phoenix Corps for help."

"Give it time. You've been through a lot."

"I can't protect them like this."

Ridge kissed her gently, his hand sifting softly through the tangles in her hair. "I already told you. I'm not going anywhere. I'll keep you all safe, if that's what it takes."

"I can't ask..."

"You didn't ask."

Ridge's hand drifted to the back of her head and lifted her, bringing a glass of cool water to her parched lips.

"Keep the water down for a bit, and we'll try some food again. Then more rest. You have a lot of injuries to heal before we are ready to worry about anything else."

The cool liquid coated her mouth and throat, and she closed her eyes as he let her head rest back on the cot. Darkness overtook her, but his warm fingers over her own kept her grounded.

As sleep threatened to pull her under, Pip's words came to mind. "You don't deserve the gift we gave you, so we're taking it back."

Agony, both physical and psychological, swelled.

"They've taken my Komodo dragon."

THE END

Thank you for joining Ridge and Karma on this adventure! There's so much more to come! Reviews are a big part of helping new readers find stories they will enjoy. I'd greatly appreciate it if you left a review for Karma's Coming.

Karma's Here, book 2 in this action-packed series, is available at books2read.com/u/4DBqwe.

What else is in store? Breaking Point showed you three areas devastated by disasters. We will visit each of them along the way. Each area will get its own duology and the characters from all the books will come together for a final book (or two) where Phoenix Corps will be confronted and more information will come to light. Find updates on this series and more at jillianbeane.com.

About Jillian

Jillian has been writing since high school. Finally published 25+ years later, she has had oodles of careers to keep her busy along the way....

Stay-at-home mom

Preschool Teaching Assistant

Licensed Journeyman Plumber

Secret Squirrel

Security for a Professional Baseball Team

Disability Adjudicator

Credit Card Fraud Investigator

Does she know what she wants to do when she grows up? Nah! Where's the surprise in that?!?!

Surrounded by the support of her loving husband, her two amazing and crazy kids, and her family, she is adding AUTHOR to her ever-growing list of careers.

When she isn't writing action-packed fantasy adventures full of found family and love, you can find her reading, watching movies, listening to music, or hanging out with her Yas at their favorite art studio getting into ALL the shenanigans. Whether creating with her words or her hands, Jillian finds joy in art of all forms, be it remodeling or building projects, crochet, painting on canvas or pottery, or simply sitting in front of the dreaded blinking cursor, preparing to go on an adventure with her imaginary friends.

Acknowledgements

First, thank you to all of you who have read this book through to the end. Thank you for coming along on this journey with me! I truly hope you enjoyed it. Hopefully there will be many more adventures together in our futures!

This book would have never been possible without the support of my amazing husband and beautiful daughters. I can never thank them enough.

To my Yas, I cannot express how much your support and cheerleading helped to get me through the imposter syndrome moments. And a special thank you to the QueenYa for all of your help in 'fixing' my attempts to create a cover, logo, bookmark, etc. and advice on my small business! As always, the covers shine after being in your masterful hands!

To my Author Ever After community, thank you for lighting the fire under me and helping to walk me through the intimidating process of self-publishing. To my WWF crew, thank you for keeping me on task... sometimes, and holding me accountable for getting words and making posts.

Also by Jillian Beane

The Elemental Series

Elements: A Moment In Time (prequel scene)

Elements: A Battle Before (prequel novella)

Elements & Flame (March 2024)

Elements & the Fae (Summer 2024)

Elements & a Key (Spring 2025)

<u>Altered Karma Series</u>

Karma's Coming (Jan 2026)

Karma's Here (Feb 2026)

Fate's Stories (2 books) *Publish Dates TBA*

Destiny's Stories (2 books) *Publish Dates TBA*

Series wrap up – *Publish Dates TBA*

www.ingramcontent.com/pod-product-compliance
Lightning Source LLC
Chambersburg PA
CBHW030151310726
48970CB00005B/1685